KATHMANDU KILLERS

AN INTERNATIONAL DETECTIVE THRILLER

LUKE RICHARDSON

1

Twenty years ago. Kent, England.

Aisha Mwangi applied the brakes and her Vauxhall Nova slowed. The engine stuttered, threatening to conk out altogether.

"Not now," she said, soothingly, acutely aware she was talking to an inanimate object. "Don't break down on me today."

Aisha glanced at the map spread out on the passenger seat. The problem was, this lane looked like all the others. Thick hedgerows, budding with spring blossom, ran down both sides of the narrow track. The only variation was that in some places trees hung right over the road completely obscuring the sky, thrusting the car into premature dusk. Aisha cruised slowly through one such tunnel of trees now.

"It's got to be around here somewhere," she said, her eyes flicking from the map to the road through the windscreen. Maybe she should have let someone come with her after all, she thought. At least they would have done a better job of reading the map than she was. But then again, today was about her and her daughter. No one else. It would be worth it when she got to see Allissa. A mixture of emotions welled inside her at the thought. It had been several months since Aisha had seen her daughter and she ached with every fiber of her soul to hold the little girl.

Aisha had never really been in a relationship with Allissa's father. In hindsight, it had been nothing more than a fleeting affair which was well over by the time she'd found out she was pregnant. At first, she wasn't sure she should tell him about the baby, but ultimately thought it was the right thing to do.

What she didn't expect was the series of court summons, sham claims about her fitness as a mother, and rumored bribes to officials which landed the child in his custody. And now, years on, Aisha struggled to even see her daughter.

Aisha gripped the wheel hard, the anger and longing which she battled constantly broiling up inside her. Suddenly, she felt as though she were about to cry. Hot tears pricked at the corners of her eyes, but Aisha fought them away. There would be time to cry later. There would be lots of crying later, that she knew for sure. Now, however, she needed to remain cool.

"It shouldn't be like this," Aisha muttered to herself. "No mother should have to go through this."

The car swept out from beneath the low-hanging trees. Aisha squinted, momentarily dazzled by the sunlight. She flipped down the sun visor, the damn thing almost falling off in her hand.

She swung around another bend and then across a narrow bridge. Aisha peered down at the bubbling stream below.

The lane twisted up to the left. Aisha applied pressure to the gas, and the Nova shuddered up the incline, belching black fumes.

"And if I'm not totally wrong, it should be just here." Aisha slowed the car to a crawl. A pair of towering iron gates appeared on the right-hand side, just as she'd thought.

"This is where you're keeping her," Aisha muttered, looking up at the menacing gates. A security camera topped one pillar.

The property's name — Stockwell Manor — glimmered on a brass plate.

The gates swung open silently, revealing a curved gravel drive.

"They must be expecting me," Aisha muttered, fighting the Nova into its lowest gear. She pulled into the driveway, sending a cloud of dust up behind her.

The driveway turned in a wide arc, and then the manor house appeared. Set on several acres of land, the place looked more abandoned than secluded. The windows were dark and forlorn, like the remains of some nuclear disaster. The dark stone facade loomed ominously against the gray sky.

Aisha gripped the wheel, her heart racing. Her stomach twisted and turned. Not just butterflies, a whole wake of vultures circled in her guts.

Aisha pulled into a large circular graveled area at the front of the house. A waterless fountain sat in the center, the carved cherubs long succumbed to the ravages of lichen.

Applying the brake, the Nova crunched to a stop. Aisha switched off the ignition. Like a mechanical sigh of thanks, the Nova coughed into silence. Aisha climbed out of the car. A chilly breeze whipped through the air, incongruous on the warm spring day. Aisha pulled her jacket tightly around her.

The wind whispered through the trees, rustling the leaves and making them seem like sinister fingers reaching out to grab her. She hesitated, wondering if she should turn back, but then she thought of Allissa. Her child. Aisha squared her shoulders, steeled her determination, and strode towards the front door.

2

Sundown in Kathmandu.

A blinding orange sun sank through a fragmented wall of clouds. Shafts of haggard, uncompromising light signaled the falling blanket of dusk. Behind the sprawling city, the silver backs of the Himalayas stood resolute.

The clang and yammer of daytime production muted as merchants, makers, and menders packed away the tools of their trade. A welder, a bicycle repairman, a tire salesman. Their work for the day was now complete, and their concern for the hunger of their families met, for now.

In the upstairs windows, lights blazed. The smell

of spice and onions replaced the odor of oil, paint, and rubber.

Two young men made their way through a backstreet. This city was a warren of such narrow thoroughfares, allowing people to scuttle unseen.

Concrete structures stood tall on both sides, leaving a narrow, dusty path. The going was difficult. The men knew it would be worth it, however. As they turned left at a crossroads, the narrow passage forced them into single file. They walked in silence.

The man in front lit a cigarette; it flared in the shadows.

The residents of the city were used to these people. A rabble of them had passed through their city, homes, and restaurants for as long as anyone could remember.

For some, it was the beginning of a journey — perhaps Pokhara, or Everest. For others, it was the end. A last stop before the road became impassable, inconvenient, or uncomfortable, and the flight home beckoned.

The men walked towards the end of the passage, a dead end — the concrete wall of a building. Its ugly construction looked bulky and mysterious in the darkness. Pipes and wires bulged like veins across its skin.

The men knew what they sought, however. They had been there before.

All they had to do was look for the light. A bare bulb, swinging on its wire and encircled by insects, hung above a door. It was the only thing that separated the door the men were seeking from any other.

The men saw the light and hurried onwards. The door opened before the men reached it. A waiter with an oily smile stood in the gloom. Nodding as they entered, the waiter showed them to a table in the dark room. The small restaurant was kept dark on purpose.

"You want the lamb? We have the lamb again," the waiter said when the men were seated. The men nodded, ordered beers, and resumed their conversation.

They were moving on the next day, out into the mountains, hiking somewhere. The waiter couldn't work out where, even in the quiet of the empty restaurant. The waiter placed bottled beers on the table; neither of the young men looked up. Then he hung back in the shadows, listening.

"Looking forward to leaving this city..." one man said to the other.

"Yeah, it's not been..."

From the scraps of conversations, the waiter made a decision.

"There are so many other places…"

"We're getting out tomorrow…"

The oily grin ran across his face as he clicked a switch on the wall. The light outside — look for the light — died into darkness.

In the restaurant, the men ate wordlessly. The lamb was as spectacular as ever. Perfectly spiced, sizzling, succulent, and fresh. They abandoned cutlery and ate with their hands, grabbing at the meat by its bones, skin, and muscle.

Although meat was served in Nepal, it wasn't the norm. The pair had been in the city a few days, and they had seen nothing like the lamb served at the backstreet restaurant.

"They get it from the mountains," they'd been told by a guy they had met on their first afternoon in the city.

"It's the best meat in Nepal, if you can find the place. The lambs live up in the mountains where they eat wild grasses and breathe the fresh air. That's what makes them so big and strong. Most restaurants here don't serve it — or save it for their best customers. This place, if you can find it, is amazing."

Later that evening, they'd followed the guy's directions down the passageways, each one smaller than the last. By some luck, they found their way to the dark door advertised only by the bare bulb.

They had been back three times since. The waiter with the oily smile had greeted them each time, and each time they had ordered the succulent, delicious Himalayan Lamb.

From the kitchen door, the waiter stood and watched. One man tore meat from a long bone with his teeth, while the other picked at it like a vulture devouring an abandoned carcass. When they'd finished eating, the waiter collected the dishes.

The men stretched backwards, resting their full stomachs. Sweat mottled their pink foreheads.

"You want our special smoke?" the waiter asked.

The men looked at each other.

"We have to catch a bus early in the morning."

"It's free because you are special customers, coming back again. It's a family tradition," the waiter insisted.

The men exchanged smiles. They were in Kathmandu. How could they refuse?

The waiter returned with a large, ornate hookah pipe. Liquid gurgled as the men drew on the pipe, inhaling the sweet spoke. The coal glowed red like the eyes of a devil.

"With our compliments," the waiter said, melting into the gloom.

3

Twenty years ago. The Stockwell Family Estate, Kent, England.

The right honorary Blake Stockwell was used to solving problems. He'd spent his whole life solving problems. Whether that was striking unions, party members that refused to tow the line, or the change of regimes that didn't flow his way, he always found a solution. He was one of life's opportunists, Stockwell liked to think. That was all there was to it. He made success, power, and money out of what other people thought was too difficult, impossible, or not worth the hassle. A member of her majesty's parliament for over a decade, he had it down to an art form.

Stockwell lifted the crystal glass to his lips and

took a deep sip of whisky. He felt the spirit fill his mouth and nose with its fragrance, then burn as it slipped down into his stomach. With that in mind, today was nothing more than he had done a thousand times over — a problem to be solved.

A heavy knock drew Stockwell's attention to the front door.

"Right on time," he muttered, sliding the glass on to the counter and pacing through into the vast hallway. He swung open the door and stared at the young African woman standing on the porch. Stockwell's eyes moved from her face down across her body, before returning to meet her gaze. She was just as beautiful as he'd remembered all those years ago.

"Aisha," Stockwell said, his voice warm. "Thank you for coming."

"Like I had a choice," Aisha said, pacing past Stockwell into the hallway. She looked around at the dark wooden-clad interior and then turned to face Stockwell. A deathly silence hung over the house. "Where is she?"

Stockwell, momentarily distracted by the beautiful woman now standing in his hallway, shook himself back into focus.

"Ah yes." Stockwell stepped towards Aisha and extended his hands, intending to touch her shoulders.

"Touch me and I'll snap your fingers off. I want to see my daughter, now."

Stockwell froze. His head tilted to one side. "You see, it's this anger problem that gets in your way. That's why she's safer with me. But I didn't bring you here to go over old ground. Come into the kitchen."

Stockwell paced past Aisha and led them into the kitchen.

Aisha stepped into the room. Although this room alone was probably the size of the entire apartment she shared with her sister, there was no life here. No children's toys scattered the floor. No finger paintings hung from the fridge door. No laughter echoed from games in other rooms. Aisha shuddered. The place was eerie.

Stockwell turned to face his guest and then leaned against the counter.

"I'm here to propose something of a truce. No child benefits from warring parents. All these court cases, solicitors' fees, time away from work — they're costly and distracting..."

"You're telling me," Aisha muttered. She'd already cleaned out her savings and was working all the shifts she could manage to keep the legal bills paid. The cost didn't seem to bother Blake Stockwell, though, with his substantial albeit lifeless country pile.

"We need to come to an arrangement, that suits us both, and most importantly... crucially... foremost... is beneficial for Allissa," Stockwell twittered on. He was not the sort of man to keep things to a few words when many more would suffice. "She's getting older now too, as you might remember..."

"As I might remember," Aisha roared, stepping forward. Every muscle ached for her to smash Stockwell in the face, right now. She stopped herself, freezing mid stride. Her jaw set into a scowl. "I know exactly how old she is, and I know exactly how many days it is since you stole her from me. I know that child better than you ever will." Aisha's right hand slid across her stomach.

"Well, yes, of course, I wasn't suggesting there's anything wrong with your memory," Stockwell said, dismissively. "Here's what I propose." He stepped across to the oak table in the middle of the room. A leather briefcase sat in the center of the table. Stockwell unclasped the locks. The snapping noise reverberated through the room.

"What I propose is a truce. A simple exchange that will benefit everyone." Stockwell lifted the lid of the briefcase. Stacks of cash were lined up inside.

Aisha's mouth made the shape of an O. She stared at the notes for a long moment and then up at the man with whom, in the best-worst decision of her life, she had created a child. Time stood still. Her heart froze mid beat.

Stockwell, unreceptive of Aisha's reaction, continued to talk. "There is one-hundred-thousand-pounds in this case. That will be, I think, more than enough for you to start a new life elsewhere. Maybe go back to Kenya, if that's what you desire. Find yourself a husband, if you want. You're still young, you can have dozens of children." While speaking these last words, Stockwell stared at Aisha. His gaze moved across her in a manner that would have forced her into rage, even without the suggestion that he could buy their child.

"No way. You sick, horrible, disgusting man," Aisha roared, her voice shaking with anger and hurt. She stalked forwards, her muscles taught, all vestiges of control gone.

"I will fight every day. With every penny I can find and every moment of my life to get my child back to where she belongs. I will fight until my dying day..."

The final words caught in Aisha's throat as Stockwell spun around. His hand grasped her neck, hard. His thick fingers dug into her flesh. He was much stronger than she'd expected and easily lifted her from the floor.

Aisha swung at him, trying to grab, slap or punch.

Kathmandu Killers

She landed a blow to the side of Stockwell's face, but that only seemed to spur him on.

Aisha felt him pull her backwards. Her feet dragged uselessly across the floor.

Stockwell hauled her out through an open door and onto a terrace at the back of the house,

Panic clouded Aisha's vision now. She was fighting for her life. She kicked and clawed, trying to work herself free from the man's grip. It was no use. He held her firm. She felt faint. Her vision clouded. Her lungs ached for the air she needed too much.

Stockwell dragged Aisha to the edge of the terrace. There, an ornate wall stood at the top of a twenty-foot drop. As though she weighed nothing, Stockwell swung Aisha across the wall.

She made another attempt to grab at him, but now all her strength was gone.

"You really should have taken the money," Stockwell growled, pulling Aisha's face in close to his. "But at least you got it your way, you fought until your dying day."

Stockwell swung the woman across the railing and out into nothing. Her arms flailed. Her face contorted into a mask of shock. Her eyes locked on his until she hit the slabs down below.

Stockwell licked his lips, then ran a hand across

his face. He turned and looked down at his as fingers. Blood streaked across his hand. He touched his face again. He was bleeding from a scratch on his cheek.

"Oh well," Stockwell muttered, wiping the finger on his trousers. "Another problem solved." Stockwell turned and walked back into the house. He now had several phone calls to make.

4

Seven months until Mya's disappearance. Brighton, England.

I'm going to kiss you now, Leo thought to himself, his confidence growing after an evening of shared drinks, smiles, and laughs with Mya. It was only the second time they had met, but it was going well.

Several hours ago, they had met at a wood-beamed pub in The Lanes. The night was busy, but Leo had hardly noticed anyone else as they moved on to a basement cocktail bar with gleaming bar stools, low lighting, and a booth at the back designed for intimate nights out.

As they stepped out into the lustrous morning air at 4 am, Mya asked, "Where to now?"

"India!" Leo shouted, uncharacteristically boisterously.

"Go on then," Mya said, giggling and putting her arm through Leo's. "Take me to India."

I'm going to kiss you now, Leo thought again, looking out at the curving domes of the Royal Pavilion floating in the milky pinks of summer pre-dawn. The tall flowers in the garden mirrored the sky with dew-covered leaves.

Sitting on a bench in the glinting air, drinking from cans, Mya wore his jacket and curved her shape into his. Leo tried not to notice the cold as his hand slipped down her back, tracing the contours of her figure beneath the dress he had been admiring all night. They had created a bubble around themselves that was theirs alone. The world had become just the two of them. This was his moment. Their moment.

As the sun warned of its impending arrival, Leo took a sip of his beer, reminding himself to breathe. "I'm going to kiss you now," he said, the words slipping out before his drunken ears had even registered them.

Mya looked up at him, her eyes absorbing the colors of the sky. The kiss was passionate, sexy, steamy, and full of longing. It was all Leo had wanted and more. Her skin was soft beneath his touch. They kissed until they were kissing more than not, lost in their own world — a planet just for them. Leo inhaled the scent of her neck as passion reached boiling point. He wanted to live in this moment forever. He didn't want it to end, but he knew it would with the rising sun.

Neither of them noticed as the light faded from purple to peach.

Leo pulled on Mya's hand — it was time to go. One more kiss as they stood up, and then the bubble burst. The world was now alive. Buses pulled sleepy passengers to work, people walked their dogs, and bikes zipped past on the way into the city.

Laughing, Leo and Mya climbed over the fence and back into the city. Reaching her apartment, Mya rummaged through her bag for the key, unlocked the door, and led Leo inside. The bed was still covered with the dresses she had laid there earlier.

As Leo gazed up at Mya, the light caught her jawline, her strong cheekbones, and her figure. Her dress slipped to the floor.

Leo's pulse raged in a mix of excitement and awe.

Mya's body was a silhouette against the light. Mya moved towards him, but he was already there, already living in the moment. They rolled like thunder into the darkness, into the silence.

Present Day. Brighton, England.

Bang, bang, bang!

A fist banged against the door of Leo's flat.

Leo groaned. It definitely wasn't time to get up yet. He ignored the noise and resettled. It was probably just the neighbor leaving. The communal staircase passed his front door and the family who lived upstairs liked to lug the stroller up and down at all times of the day or night. In fact, Leo's apartment was constructed in such a way that he could hear every noise the people upstairs made, especially in the kitchen.

Leo had settled again, when the noise returned. This time banging didn't stop. It didn't just sound as though someone was trying to get his attention, but that they were trying to break through the door completely.

"Fine," Leo muttered, opening his eyes. He lifted his head and looked around. He wasn't in bed. In front of his unfocused eyes, the two screens of his computer glowed. Rain hammered against the window. Leo rubbed his face and stretched. *What time is it?*

He glanced at the clock on the screen. 6 am. The milky half-light through the curtainless window confirmed this. The new day would soon be here, whether Leo liked it or not.

The barrage of knocking came again, threatening to split the thin wood of Leo's front door.

"Okay, okay," Leo groaned, climbing shakily to his feet. "I'm coming." It was probably a parcel. Those delivery people really did get insistent.

Leo padded across the threadbare carpet of his front room and into the hallway. He snapped on the light and turned to face the door. Through the frosted glass panel, Leo could see a dark shape standing in the hallway.

If Leo had known what this early morning visitor would bring into his life, then maybe he'd have thought twice about opening the door. But, of course, he didn't know then. At that moment Leo was an unemployed journalist still hung up in the disappearance of his former girlfriend. He knew nothing of Blake Stockwell, his daughter Allissa, or the city of Kathmandu.

"This parcel guy is clearly going for employee of the month."

Without another thought, Leo unlocked the door and pulled it open.

"Leo Keane?" The man standing in the hallway grunted.

Leo looked up at the man. Still half-asleep, his vision didn't focus at first. The visitor was a big man. Actually, a giant among men. His neck was probably the width of Leo's waist and his arms looked as though he worked out by lifting family cars.

"Yes," Leo said, instantly wondering whether that was the right thing to do.

"You've got a visitor," the man said, his tone hard.

"Well, obviously,"

"I need to come inside." It wasn't a question. The man pushed forward and with an open palm the size of a snow shovel. Leo stepped aside, just in time.

Once inside, the man glanced around, assessing the apartment with the hard concentration of someone who'd learned such diligence the hard way.

"No cameras or recording devices in here?" the man said.

"Urmm, no."

"Phones, tablets, laptops?"

"All in the front room." Leo pointed to his desk in the front room. He wondered to himself why he was being so compliant with the guy, then once again looked at the mountain of muscle which now stood in front of him.

The man produced what looked like a hand-held metal detector and ran it over the surface of Leo's

Kathmandu Killers

clothes. If he had any opinion on the stained joggers and hoody, he didn't share it.

"This searches for recording devices. Top of the range kit. Can detect a bug from six feet," the man said, without Leo asking. The man stepped into the kitchen and spun around, swinging the device as though he was conducting an orchestra. "It's clear," he said into an unseen radio. "You can send The Lord up." The man turned to Leo. "You'll speak to The Lord in the kitchen. I'll be waiting out here. It should only take a few minutes, and then we will be out of your way."

5

Present Day. Kathmandu, Nepal.

Sometimes in life, you just have to run.

Fuli had passed the door many times whilst she'd been kept in the house. She'd noticed the outside world glinting mysteriously through the glass, but had never thought to try the handle. Until today.

She knew he was expecting her in the back room. He'd shouted for her to come down only moments ago. He'd be expecting her to come through the curtain soon.

He'd be having a hushed conversation with the man who'd just arrived. They'd be acting like old friends, talking about her, and exchanging piles of dirty money. All of that would stop, replaced by false smiles as she entered.

Fuli knew what would happen behind the curtain. She'd been there often enough.

She had despised it in the beginning. The cold, callused touch of the sort of men that arrived made her skin crawl. But then she grew used to it — the idle chatter, the commands, her compliance. A few minutes after, time would be hers again. Some took longer than others, but none took that long.

Today could be different, she thought, holding the door open. The fresh breeze of the afternoon streamed in. She had felt the breeze many times before from behind the bars of her third-floor window. It was never this intoxicatingly close.

"Fuli, get in here!" came his voice, rough and rank from smoking and whisky. She knew the smell. He kept her for himself sometimes when he'd had too much. "Don't keep your visitor waiting." It sounded as if he were smiling. He was probably sharing a joke, counting the visitor's money and telling him dirty things about her.

Fuli teetered with the possibility. She could close the door again. No one would ever know she'd even thought about it. Or she could try her luck out there.

It isn't that bad here, she thought, high on opportunity but scared of unfamiliarity. She was one of the lucky ones, he'd said, one of his favorites. Others forced their girls to do all sorts of things. He had rules, though. He respected her and made sure her visitors did too.

Fuli remembered what it was like when she'd first been brought here. She thought about his hot and sour breath against her face for the first time. That was months ago now, even years. Fuli remembered it though — as clear as the traffic through the gap in the door. She remembered sitting on the stained mattress in the room upstairs after he had finished with her. He liked to be the first. That's what he'd said.

"Get down here now." His voice was aggressive now. He'd moved closer to the curtain which obscured the back room from the door.

Fuli peered through the gap, invigorated at the possibility. The traffic noise swirled around her. The smell of fumes was noxious and exciting. A brightly colored bus pulled near. Enthusiastic people gazed through the smeared windows. All of them going somewhere. People visiting their families, or tourists going hiking in the mountains. Wherever they were going, they were excited and happy. Free. They were not confined to a dirty mattress in a dark room, waiting for his call.

As the bus pulled closer, Fuli noticed a group of Nepali men through the front window. They spoke excitedly, with animated expressions. Maybe it was their first journey together — *a journey she deserved too.*

Fuli stepped through the door, towards grumbling traffic and the potent smell of the city. She felt the bright daylight warm her skin. She glanced nervously over her shoulder and pulled the door closed behind her.

Fuli squinted against the bright afternoon sun as she took her first steps of freedom. The surrounding street thronged with bikes, taxis, and cars. It felt a million miles from the small village in which she grew up.

"What are you doing? Get back here!"

He must have heard the door shut behind her. His voice sounded different outside — distant, yet still angry and worse, dangerous. She didn't want to go back. She couldn't go back. She ran.

She turned left and then right without daring to look behind her. She didn't want to see his outstretched arms, ready to take her back to that house, that room, those men.

Fuli ran towards a crowd of people ahead. Her feet

ached. Her thin shoes were no match for the turbulent road. She overtook slowing cars and dived into a crowded market. She pushed past people, only hearing their protests as she passed. One more reason not to stop. She couldn't stop now.

She had to keep going.

6

Present Day. Brighton, England.

Leo paced into the kitchen and clicked on the kettle. He peered out of the window. Although rain pounded against the glass, the sky was lightening. Winter was coming, and the flat was getting cold. Leo rubbed his hands together, then did up the zipper on his hoody. He glanced at the boiler. He should put the heating on, but since he'd lost his job, paying the bills had become problematic.

Steam curled from the kettle as it rattled to the boil and clicked off. Leo dumped half a tablespoon of instant coffee in a cup, added a splash of milk, and filled it with the boiling water.

Footsteps shuffled on the stairs behind him, and then another voice filled the hallway.

"Mr. Keane," came an aristocratic voice from the kitchen door. "Thank you for seeing me like this. I realize it's all a bit sudden. I told Giles to treat you with the utmost respect."

Leo turned to see a large man step into the kitchen. He wore a dark pinstriped suit, which Leo thought probably cost more than the combined contents of his apartment. A mop of graying hair indicated the man was probably in his late sixties, although Leo couldn't be sure. The man also sounded quite out of breath after climbing the stairs. The kitchen door slammed shut, leaving Leo alone with his unwanted guest.

"Please, let me introduce myself. I'm Blake Stockwell. You may have heard of me, former Member of Parliament, now I sit in the House of Lords."

Sure enough, Leo had heard of the man. Working at the local newspaper, he'd written several articles on Lord Stockwell's various scrapes and misdemeanors. Leo hoped this visit wasn't about one of them.

"Oh coffee, excellent, thanks," Stockwell said, picking up the steaming cup from the counter. He removed a hip flask from inside his jacket and poured some of the contents into the cup.

"It's medicinal, would you like a drop?"

Leo shook his head and then retrieved another cup from the draining board and set about making another coffee.

"I don't mean to be forward, Lord Stockwell," Leo said.

"Blake, please," Stockwell cooed.

"Why are you in my kitchen?"

"Now that's an excellent question, young man." Stockwell took a greedy sip of the coffee. "Let me get straight to the point. I can see you're a busy man. You find missing people, right?"

Leo turned and looked at the Lord. There was no sign that the man was anything but serious.

"No, I'm afraid I don't. You must have me confused with someone else."

"You set up and run the website Missing People International, don't you?" Stockwell countered.

"That's correct, yes."

Leo had set up the website after his girlfriend, Mya had disappeared over two years ago. The website combined several resources he found helpful in his search for her, including a feature which notified the user if the missing person appeared in anything posted online. Leo still had it running in his search for Mya. The search included the locations she wanted to visit, carefully chosen keywords and a more general description. It had been running non-stop for almost two years but had got him nowhere.

"Then, I think it's fair to say that you find missing people."

Although I've never found anyone, not least Mya, Leo thought, keeping the negativity to himself.

"Well listen, now we've cleared that up, I need your help. It concerns my daughter. My youngest, Allissa." Stockwell had a way of speaking that made the whole lower part of his face wobble. "She's always been a problem to us, never wanted to do any of the things the other girls did. We sent her to the best schools, and she did well but was never interested in using her qualifications. She's got this idea in her head about trying to change the world. The more we spent on her education, the more she used it to rail against us." He paused and sipped the coffee. "I mean, I'm no monster, but I just don't see the appeal for a young, beautiful, intelligent girl to help a bunch of people who're doing nothing to help themselves."

"I understand." Leo wondered whether him helping Stockwell would be exactly that.

"Good. Well, it all came to a head two years ago. She'd graduated from Cambridge. Did very well. Written a thesis about some socialist nonsense, but it was good, apparently. Anyway, Eveline, my wife, secured her a contract at a local law firm. The perfect opportunity. Would've got her career off to a flying start. We knew she was reluctant, but thought it was just nerves, and that she'd be alright once she got started. Anyway, a couple of weeks before her graduation, she just disappeared. No goodbye. No nothing."

Stockwell lifted the drink to his lips again. His face reddened with each swallow.

"Eveline was distraught. I thought Allissa would be back in a couple of weeks. Allissa had always been argumentative, as I said, but she'd never actually left before. We got a call a few days later, when she told us she was going traveling for a bit. Going to see a bit of the world, that kind of thing. She had access to a savings account with a fair amount of money in it. Not that much, but I'm told it was enough to live a basic lifestyle for some time."

"Do you know where she went?"

"South America or Asia, somewhere like that." Stockwell grimaced.

"Do you know where she is now?"

"Well, we've heard nothing for over a year. She's over eighteen, so we can't track her accounts. A couple of months ago she called, quite out of the blue, and asked her sister to transfer a large sum of money from a trust fund into a Nepalese account in Kathmandu. Thirty-five grand..."

Leo's eyes widened.

"Lucy, her sister, transferred the money before telling us. That was the deal Allissa had made with her. Allissa said she didn't mind us knowing after the transfer had been made." Stockwell drained the cup. "Obviously, we were relieved to know she was safe." His voice became an angry crescendo. "But... I mean, what could she possibly be doing with thirty-five grand?"

Leo shook his head. "How can I help you with this? Surely you can look online?"

"No, we've tried that. Nothing. The more we look, the more worried we become. Kathmandu seems to be full of all sorts of unsavory people. No telling what they do out there. They're savages." Stockwell pointed a ham-colored finger at Leo. "I want you to go and find her. Find our Allissa."

Leo felt a bolt of anxiety twist in his chest. Sure, he'd traveled before, but that was with Mya. She'd known what she was doing. She made it easy for him. His chest tightened.

"Obviously, we'd pay for your time and costs. This is very important to us."

The money would certainly be useful now that

Leo didn't have a job, but this wasn't his thing. He wasn't a detective. Leo focused harder on his breathing as the anxiety took hold.

"Shall we say ten grand upfront and five more when you arrive?"

Leo's chest tightened further at the thought. Sure, looking online, Leo could do that. But going to an unknown city on the other side of the world...

Leo stuttered an answer. He took a deep breath and composed himself.

"You know, Lord Stockwell... Blake. I'd love to help you. But I'm not a detective." Leo took a sip of the coffee. "I'm just someone who's lost someone, too. I try to help other people in any way I can." He paused. One quick inhale. One slow exhale. "But I've never gone and actually looked for them."

"I think you've misinterpreted me... Leo." Stockwell pronounced the name as though it might break. "I may not agree with all the decisions my daughter has made, but I am her father, and I am concerned for her safety. I cannot rest thinking she might be involved in something horrible over there." His face contorted with displeasure. "I... I mean, we, my wife and I — our whole family — we just want her home, or at least to know she's safe."

Watching Stockwell struggle over the words, Leo

felt an understanding. He knew what it was like to need answers. If it were Mya in Kathmandu, then Leo knew he'd go in an instant. Leo thought about Mya's insatiable thirst for adventure. She had a never-ending desire for new and exciting experiences. Leo took another sip of the coffee and felt the possibilities start a fire of willingness. A fire that quickly took hold.

He needed the money too.

"If you'll do it..." Stockwell paused, watching Leo's conflict like a snake ready for lunch. "If you do it, that would be great. I really want you to. If you can't... well, I'll find someone else who will."

"Okay, I'll" — Leo heard the words before he knew he was saying them — "I'll do it."

Watching Lord Stockwell, Leo tried to work out if the unnatural exposure of his teeth was supposed to be a grin.

Stockwell turned and tapped on the kitchen door. The beefy security guard opened the door and passed through a dark leather briefcase. Stockwell placed the case on the kitchen counter, unlocked it, and rummaged through the contents. He removed a yellow folder and passed it to Leo.

"In here is everything you'll need. Copies of recent photographs. A description of her. Details of her interests." He closed the briefcase and placed it on the floor, glaring at the counter as though it might infect the case with its filthiness.

Leo opened the folder and slipped out four typed sheets of paper and two photographs. The first page contained the details that Stockwell had just mentioned. Leo turned over the page and saw the first of the pictures. To Leo's surprise, the image that stared back at him looked nothing like Stockwell. Allissa was beautiful. She had a bright smile and radiant eyes. In contrast to the large man that sat in front of him, she had dark skin. Leo looked from the picture to Stockwell and back again. There were similarities, but Allissa obviously got her complexion from her mother.

"How many children do you have?" Leo asked, looking up at Stockwell.

Stockwell sat up a little straighter at the question. "Two daughters and one son."

Leo asked a couple more questions, and each time Stockwell answered them simply.

"The more I know," Leo said, "the better understanding I'll have of Allissa. That'll help me find her."

Leo looked back at the picture and realized why Stockwell had chosen it. This must be the mental image he had of his daughter. In the picture, a relaxed

Allissa walked through a field, as though on a country-side stroll.

Leo turned over to the next picture.

"She sent this one to her sister about a year ago," Stockwell said, watching Leo myopically.

In this photograph, Allissa sat on a beach looking over her shoulder at the camera. To Leo, it felt more like the sort of picture Allissa would choose of herself. She looked healthy, happy, and free. Behind her, a deserted beach rolled into palm groves. Her dark hair fell over her shoulders. Her skin was clear and glowing.

"It's the most recent photograph we have. I wasn't going to include it, but Eveline said I should."

"She looks happy in it," Leo told him. "It's a nice picture."

Stockwell grumbled and looked at his watch. "I'll leave that with you." Stockwell pulled a checkbook and pen from his jacket pocket. He filled in the check, then held it out for Leo. "Ten thousand pounds. Send me your account details, and I'll wire you the rest when you touch down."

Leo looked at the check in Stockwell's extended grasp. The gold embossed letters of the bank's unusual logo glimmered.

"I want updates every two days," Stockwell said.

Kathmandu Killers

"Don't think you can sit around and still get paid." His eyes narrowed harshly as Leo reached for the check.

"I'll be out there looking for your daughter," said Leo. "However, do be aware I may not find her. I'll need to be paid either way."

Stockwell held on the check for a long, uncomfortable moment and considered Leo through narrowed eyes. "Oh, you'll get paid," Stockwell finally said. "Don't worry about that."

7

Present Day. Kathmandu, Nepal.

"Namaste. How are you?" Allissa Stockwell said, practicing the Nepalese she'd been learning. Her mouth stumbled over the unfamiliar words.

The market seller sitting cross-legged behind a pyramid of tomatoes smiled in surprise.

"I'm fine but hot," he replied, his eyes turning towards the bright afternoon sky.

Allissa beamed — she'd been understood, although his answer was lost on her.

The market bustled around her. Within this small area, the sprawling concrete of the city was replaced by strips of colored cloth stacked with spices, vegetables, fruit and flowers.

Watching the other browsers, Allissa knelt, picked a tomato from the pile, then brought it close to her face and inhaled the sweet fragrance. It had taken most of her life and half the world to know how to take her time.

In England, where she'd grown up, people always wanted to be somewhere else and never actually enjoyed where they were. In the last two years, Allissa had realized how that attitude strained the simple pleasures from life. The texture of tomatoes ripening in the sun. The smell of the spices at the next stall, spoonfuls of which the seller would deposit onto a large, hollowed rock and crush and mix to the buyer's specification.

Time was ultimately all anyone had; it was what you did with it that mattered.

The distant sound of traffic grumbled behind the chatter of negotiation.

"Just these," Allissa said, dropping six tomatos into her bag. The seller tilted his head from side to side as he calculated his first price. Agreeing on a sale here involved a negotiation of several minutes. It was one custom Allissa had grown to enjoy during her time in Asia.

Two minutes later, she slid a collection of coins into the seller's outstretched hand and stepped into the stream of people. She still needed onions, spices, and yoghurt for their meal tonight.

Allissa paused at a stall of incense to breathe in the scent of sandalwood. The seller offered her the burning stick. Allissa accepted the stick and took a deep breath. She heard shouting voices from behind her. Running footsteps hammered against the ground. Something hit Allissa hard, knocking the air out of her chest.

"Watch out!" came a shout from somewhere nearby, a moment too late.

Allissa turned around, trying to make sense of what was around her. She couldn't focus on anything. The next thing Allissa knew, she was flying sideways. Her bag fell, thumping to the floor. She reached out, trying to grab hold of something to stop her fall. Her fingers swung uselessly through the air. She felt hard and heavy to the ground. A sharp pain jarred through her hip and elbow. Fortunately, her head didn't hit the concrete, leaving her hearing unaffected.

Feet rushed all around her. Voices shouted, intensifying into a crescendo. A thick hand reached down and helped her up slowly. The shouting died away, followed by comments of complaint.

Allissa glanced around. Onions bounced and skittered across the floor. In the centre of the chaos, a young woman lay sprawled out on the concrete beside her.

Allissa dusted herself down and crouched beside the woman. "Are you okay?" she said, losing all concern for herself. "Are you hurt?"

The girl stared at Allissa without understanding. Allissa's lessons in Nepalese were coming up short. She recognized the instinctive, pleading look of fear in the girl's expression. Allissa would recognize that look anywhere.

"Mānisakō, Mānisakō." The girl pointed frantically in the direction she'd come: *the man, the man.*

Allissa stood and looked around. It took her just a second to find the man the girl was running from. Across the market, next to the stuttering traffic, a large Nepalese man scanned the crowd. The way he moved told Allissa he wasn't there to shop.

Allissa glimpsed pure fear in the young woman's expression and made a decision.

"This way." Allissa pulled the girl by the arm. "Keep low."

The market had returned to normal after the disruption now. Shoppers continued to shuffle from stall to stall. The sound of chatter and negotiation drifted over the ubiquitous rumble of traffic.

Ducking down, and pushing between people,

Allissa and the young woman made their way to the opposite side of the market. Allissa pulled them through a row of stalls, muting merchants' complaints with a smile. They ducked in behind a fabric seller's display.

Peering out between two colorful drapes, Allissa saw the man shoving through the market. People scowled at him as it pushed shoppers and sellers aside. With taut muscles visible beneath his discolored white t-shirt, he looked like trouble. The man paused, looked left and right, and then continued past where Allissa and the woman were tucked out of sight.

Breathing a sigh of relief, Allissa hailed a taxi and helped the woman inside.

Ten minutes later, the woman sat on the end of Allissa's bed.

Filtered by long net curtains, the late afternoon light poured through the window. Darkness was some hours off, but the shadows had elongated toward the evening.

"I'm Allissa," Allissa said, pointing at herself, in case she'd got the translation wrong. "What's your name?"

"Fuli," the woman replied, pointing at herself.

"Excellent. It's lovely to meet you Fuli." Allissa pointed at the scrape on Fuli's shin. "I should probably get that cleaned up." Fuli extended her leg while Allissa carefully cleaned the wound.

Fuli's face was streaked where the tears had fallen. Now her eyes were dry and emotionless. With her chin resting on her hand, Fuli looked like a picture of childlike innocence. Allissa didn't think the woman could be older than twenty. She didn't know how to ask someone's age in Nepalese.

"There you are, that's looking much better," Allissa said, standing up and examining her handiwork. The wound certainly looked cleaner. Fuli offered a weak smile.

"When Chimini gets home," Allissa said, ignoring the fact she knew the girl wouldn't understand, yet afraid to let the silence go too far, "she'll explain everything. We'll talk. It'll be good to get to know you. The most important thing is that you know you're safe here."

A metallic ding drew Allissa's attention to the door. Allissa lived and worked in a small guesthouse which she was refurbishing ready to accept paying guests.

"I'll be right back," Allissa said. "You're totally safe here."

Allissa hurried out through the door and into the small reception area. A young man stood at the reception desk. He was tanned and held his rucksack easily across one shoulder.

"Hi, can I help you?" Allissa said, crossing the room.

"Yes, hi. I'm looking for a room tonight. I just got here and saw your sign outside."

"We've got nothing available tonight, I'm sorry," Allissa said without checking the register. They still needed to buy furniture for the tourists' rooms. "I am sorry. Try downstairs."

"No problem. Will do," the man said, turning back towards the stairs. The guesthouse occupied just one floor of a building above a similar operation downstairs.

"Just someone looking to see if they could stay here," Allissa said out loud as she pushed the bedroom door open. "But we've not got any room. I need to —"

She looked into the bedroom and stopped. The girl had gone.

8

Present day. Brighton, England.

One of the wonderful things about living by the sea are the sunsets, particularly on the white-fronted terraces that line Brighton's streets. The buildings reflect every strand of pink and orange and turquoise that the sinking sun projects as it drags itself beneath the horizon.

On an occasional evening, when the banks of clouds have congealed across the rambling city, it appears like there'll be no sunset at all. Sometimes on these evenings, though, something special happens. At the last minute, the flailing sun passes a crease in the cloud and pours light through. It bounces over the sea and across the white-fronted buildings with their closed windows and wet slate tiles before disappearing again as quickly as it came.

After meeting with Stockwell and agreeing to the job, Leo took his usual run along the seafront. Today he felt as though he needed it more than ever.

The nervous part of him didn't want to leave home at all. It didn't want to go anywhere. That cowardly part wanted to grovel for his job back at the local newspaper and sit behind the safe glare of his computer screens. That way, he knew what he was dealing with. That way he didn't have to come up against people he didn't trust and places he didn't know.

Yet, Stockwell had given him ten thousand pounds, just as a down payment.

Leo looked out over the sea and tried to think of a time he'd made a decision like this before. His mind drew a blank. He couldn't think of a single occasion when he had actually decided to do anything for himself.

Leo knew that, to an extent, his lifestyle was a decision. He'd rejected the graduate schemes, pension plans and homeownership ideals of many people his age. But, that felt as if it were the way things had turned out — not a decision he'd made.

He wasn't even sure how he'd ended up being a

Kathmandu Killers

journalist. Sure, he'd read a lot, and he enjoyed writing. But that was a tiny part of his half political, half promotional job at *The Echo*.

Was this trip his first proper opportunity to do something different?

The thought filled Leo with excitement. He now had something to plan, something to sort. He'd have to book flights, arrange accommodation, research the city, and come up with ideas for what he was going to do when he got there.

And yet, he didn't know the first thing about finding missing people. He didn't know the language, the local customs, the places that someone might visit. He'd never been to Nepal himself. Even if he planned it all, the idea of being successful was impossible to believe. It was all so far removed from the darkening promenade that it felt like a dream.

Who was he to think he could do this? This wasn't a job for some out-of-work journalist. Yes, he knew a bit about finding people. And yet, so far, he hadn't found anyone.

At that moment, an inch above the horizon, the sun broke through a crack in the clouds. Leo looked toward it as the sky filled with light. Every eddy and bump of the swirling grey glimmered in the dying light. Even the gulls streaking above sparkled as they cut through the low hanging clouds.

Leo narrowed his eyes to slits against the spray and pushed harder along the promenade.

Anxiety or not, whether it got him closer to Mya or not, this was his decision. Maybe the first proper decision he'd ever made.

With stinging legs and the cold, wet air of winter filling his lungs, Leo knew it was the right thing to do.

9

Chimini crossed between the skeletal trees of the square and glanced up at the guesthouse. The building shone bright amid the long shadows of the late afternoon sun. She smiled. The place had started to feel like home.

She pulled a key from her pocket and held it toward the door. The cool metal felt important and hopeful. It was the first time she'd ever had a key to anything. She slid the key into the lock, pushed open the door and stepped inside.

The last few weeks had been a whirlwind. Finding the place, negotiating with the owner, and finally getting the keys. Now all they needed was the furniture. Then the guesthouse could support themselves and anyone else in need.

"Mānisakō, Mānisakō, Mānisakō."

Chimini closed the door and the rumble of city muted behind the glass. She heard an unusual noise and stopped.

"Mānisakō, Mānisakō, Mānisakō."

It came from nearby.

"Mānisakō."

It was a female voice. Nothing more than a whisper.

Chimini tried the door to the ground floor guesthouse. That was locked.

Then she saw movement under the stairs.

"Mānisakō."

Chimini peered into the gap beneath the stairs. A girl sat against the wall, her hands placed behind her head. She rocked gently forwards and backwards.

"Mānisakō," she whispered to herself.

"Hello?" Chimini said. "Are you okay?"

The girl didn't reply. Chimini crawled into the space and sat beside the girl.

"I live upstairs," she said, after thirty seconds silence. "Do you want to come up there with me. It's safe and we can relax awhile."

The girl looked at Chimini with large, dark eyes. She said nothing. Finally, she nodded.

"Let's go up," Chimini said, helping the girl to her

feet and starting towards the stairs. "We will sit down and see if we can help you."

"Mānisako?"

"No, there are no men there. Just Allissa and me."

"Allissa?" the girl questioned, taking a step towards Chimini. "I have met Allissa."

"That's great then. You already know what to expect. Come on."

ALLISSA CHECKED THE ROOMS, the bathrooms and the storage spaces. Now she was running out of ideas. If the girl had left, had gone outside and run away, there wasn't much she could do.

Allissa crouched to look beneath the final bed. Nothing. Empty. The girl would be a few streets away by now. Allissa sat down and grumbled. This city was a dangerous place for vulnerable women. That's why she was setting up this guesthouse. It was supposed to be a safe place for those who desperately needed it — not a place they'd run away from.

Allissa rubbed her hands across her eyes. She hoped the girl had found somewhere safe to go. It hurt to see someone who needed help leave. They couldn't help everyone, though. That would never be possible.

Allissa heard voices coming from the reception area. *Chimini must be home.* Allissa listened closely and heard Chimini talking to someone in the tonal rhythms of Chimini's native Nepalese.

"Allissa?" Chimini called out.

"In here," Allissa called back.

"I found this young lady downstairs." Chimini appeared at the door with the girl beside her.

Allissa smiled and exhaled with relief.

"This is our guesthouse," Allissa explained once they were sat around the table in their small kitchen a few minutes later. "Chimini and I live here. There used to be another girl, but she got her own place last week. She'll be coming back to help us when we get up and running."

Fuli nodded.

"How long have you been here?" Allissa asked.

"I do not know," Fuli said, staring blankly.

Allissa reached across the table and touched Fuli's hand. Fuli turned and looked at Allissa.

"You're going to be safe here," Allissa said. "You can stay as long as you need."

10

Flying in across the valley, Leo had peered nervously from the bouncing plane. Below, the snow-capped mountains surrounded a sprawling city. From the air, it almost looked as though the whole place was sinking into boggy earth.

Looking down at the city, Leo found the sheer scale of the place daunting. So was the idea he was looking for someone who may not be here. He needed to look all the same.

Leo's long flight across continents had started multiple hours ago at London Gatwick. He'd queued next to a pale, dreadlocked man who looked totally out of place in the modern veneer of the terminal.

Harboring an innate fear of missing flights, he'd arrived many hours early. Unable to find anywhere to sit, Leo pushed his bag against a wall and lowered himself on top of it. Next to him, a quick-fingered Asian man packed and repacked the same suitcase. The operation was supervised by two women who muttered comments Leo didn't understand yet was sure weren't helpful.

The first thing Leo noticed about Kathmandu was the taste. It rushed into the plane as the door swung open. Leo didn't like it, yet he knew that to the million residents of the mountain city, it was the smell of opportunity.

Pushing through the noisy, humid, tussle and scrum of the airport, the part of Leo that wanted to go home screamed louder than ever. The threat of the unknown, looming large and fearful, weighed on his mind while the straps of his backpack cut into his shoulders. The pressure of his task pressed down on him like a physical weight. To find Allissa he had to get out amongst the lives and experiences of people in the city. He would have to ask questions and likely chase many shadows in pursuit of Allissa Stockwell.

Leo stumbled through the doors, dazzled by the daylight. He hailed a taxi. A small, filthy, pink and white car pulled up beside him. Leo pushed his bag inside and climbed in beside it, never letting go of the straps. The green digital clock on the dash informed

Leo that the time was five in the afternoon. To Leo, it felt like the middle of the night. He supposed probably it was. He needed to find his hotel and eat proper food on solid ground, then get some sleep.

"To The Best Kathmandu Guesthouse," Leo said. The driver examined him in the rearview mirror without responding.

"The, Best, Kathmandu, Guesthouse," Leo said again, slowly. The driver tilted his head to the side.

Leo exhaled. This was going to be more difficult than he'd anticipated.

"The... Best..." he started, sounding each word as though his pronunciation was at fault.

The driver snapped the flimsy gear stick forward, kicked the accelerator, and sent the car screeching from the curb. Leo fell backward into the worn seats and searched for the seatbelt and buckle.

The pitch and ferocity of the engine grew until it sounded as though it were on the brink of explosion. Leo peered up from the back seat. Nose to tail traffic clogged the road in both directions. The driver's knuckles whitened against the steering wheel and his head whipped from side to side.

Engines screeched as horns screamed.

A gap in the traffic appeared, and the driver accelerated for it. Violent vibrations threatened to split the small car in two. With another cacophony of horns, they slipped into the gap with inches to spare. The taxi slowed, narrowly avoiding the car in front, and Leo slid down into the footwell.

He scrambled back up to the seat and checked for the seatbelt again. He couldn't find one.

The city looked the same from the car as it had from the air. An ungainly, untidy concrete mass of buildings. Most buildings were no higher than a few stories, but seemingly endless in their number.

What couldn't be seen from the plane, though it was obvious to Leo now, was the life that inhabited the city. Every inch of the city was alive, an organic mass of moving, working parts. Each tiny shop or business spilled out into the street. Leo noticed a welder, a motorbike mechanic, and what looked like a pot maker spinning clay on a wheel all plying their trade on the same street.

Traffic engulfed the taxi on all sides. Overladen lorries rumbled past, people leaned from the windows of buses, and a pair of donkeys pulled a cart loaded with bottled water. In the centre of the melee, Leo's pink and white taxi honked and revved like a terrier taking on pack of wolves.

Having visited India with Mya, Leo thought he was

prepared for Nepal. But doing it on his own felt different. And this time he had a job to do.

The doubts swarmed his mind. How would he know who to trust? What if the taxi driver took him to the wrong place? What if someone tried to rob him? Tourists were known to carry cash and expensive things. Would Leo's pale complexion make him a likely target?

Leo's fists tightened. What if this taxi driver robbed him now? Leo could probably overpower the small driver, but if the driver knew other people — of course he knew other people — Leo knew he wouldn't stand a chance.

Leo chest tightened with the familiar tug of anxiety.

Breathing quickened.

Calm, focus, breathe.

He tried to bring the feeling under control.

Leo thought of Mya and the taxi ride they'd shared from the airport in Mumbai — Leo's first experience of India. They'd come through a similar airport scrum and into the wet heat of the Indian summer. In that first taxi ride from the airport, Leo felt as if he'd learned more about the diversity of human existence than ever before. Just outside the brand new airport terminal of marble and chrome, slums sprawled as far as Leo could see. A series of seemingly disconnected images flashed past: cars, lorries, bikes, a motorway. Cows, chickens, pigs. Children playing. Men working. Women working. People washing in pots on the side of the road, then relieving themselves next to those same pots. Women making breakfast. Old men sitting and watching the world fly by.

Four days had elapsed between Leo's meeting with Stockwell and the moment he walked through the doors of The Best Kathmandu Guesthouse.

Leo had booked the guesthouse two days ago. He'd wanted to be sparing with money, and despite the auspicious name, The Best Kathmandu Guesthouse was cheap. Although Leo had the first payment from Stockwell, he didn't know if he would ever see the rest of the money. The fact he didn't have a job on his return was constantly on his mind.

Leo had also researched his destination. He wanted to try and understand what would bring a young woman like Allissa here. What he found was a thriving, historic city steeped in Buddhist and Hindu history. Several sacred temples and monasteries had stood resolute through the change of centuries and empires and withstood many earthquakes. Leo made a note to visit these places if he had the chance. *It would be a shame to miss the culture,* he'd thought in an uncharacteristic surge of positivity.

"Welcome to The Best Kathmandu Guesthouse," came a voice from behind the reception desk. "A nice day I am wishing you." A man in an immaculate brown uniform smiled at Leo. Leo returned the greeting as energetically as he could.

After completing the check-in process, involving Leo's details being manually entered into a large ledger, the man carried Leo's bag up to his room. The man reached the room on the sixth floor without breaking a sweat. Despite carrying nothing, Leo was out of breath. After dropping the bag on the bed, the receptionist turned on the ceiling fan, mimed the use of the bathroom, then let himself out. As his footsteps drew away, Leo sat down and looked around the modest room.

The journey had been long and arduous, but Leo had arrived. This brought little relief, however, as now his real work would begin.

Leo lay back on the lumpy mattress, shut his eyes, and tried to ignore images of the taxi drivers, uneaten plane food and inescapable waiting rooms that began to drift through his mind.

11

———————

"But how come the princess always ends up with a man at the end?" Chimini asked, closing the book on the table of the guesthouse's small kitchen.

"That's just how these stories go," Allissa said, stirring the steaming pot and adding more turmeric.

"Are they saying it is important to have a guy to be happy? I don't think there are any princes here."

"You don't need to think about it in that much detail," Allissa said, turning from the stove. "I just saw the books in the market and thought of you. Not because you love princes, but because you might want something to practice reading in English."

Chimini looked through the pile of brightly colored books on the table and muttered to Fuli sitting beside her. Allissa had been helping Chimini improve her English over the last few months, but reading it was still a challenge.

"Well, if that is the case, I need to get you something to read in Nepalese." Chimini smiled.

"Yes, definitely," Allissa said, turning back to the food to hide her frown. The thought of reading the curved script of Nepali writing felt like climbing a mountain. "I'd love to," she said, gazing into the bubbling liquid.

Chimini flicked through a different book with colorful pictures. She held it up so Fuli could see. "In this one, the princess looks so unhappy until the prince comes along. Miserable! Like there is nothing to her life. It is..." She searched for the word.

"Boring?"

"Yes, it looks like she is very bored before she meets this man."

"Well, if you don't like them..." Allissa said, beaming at the women.

"No, no, I like them. I am just wondering, where is the one where the princess gets so bored of bad men, she thinks life on her own is better?"

"Well, let's write our own," Allissa said, stifling a laugh as Chimini translated for Fuli. "The food is ready, I think."

Neither girl responded. Chimini's eyes darted from

Allissa to the books, her mouth hidden behind the palm of her hand as she whispered to Fuli. Fuli's face melted into a smile.

"What are you saying about me?" Allissa said, pointing the wooden spoon toward them.

"Nothing!" Chimini replied, whispering again. Fuli laughed.

"Tell me now, or there'll be trouble." Allissa took on the deep voice of a fairy tale villain.

"No, I will never tell you!" Chimini shouted, feigning fear, then winking at Fuli. "We will never tell you..."

"Right, that's it..." Allissa took a step toward the giggling women.

"Okay... okay..." Chimini said, recovering herself from the fit of laughter. "We think you are the princess."

Shrieks and laughs echoed through the guesthouse as darkness fell across the city.

Residents scuttled home passing tourists on the way to the city's bars and restaurants. Some of these tourists may have heard the legend of the restaurant advertised only by the bare bulb. They may be making their way down the warren of reducing passages already, hoping to try the Himalayan Lamb.

12

Leo awoke in the dark. He was disorientated. At first, he thought he must have shut the curtains before going to sleep. Then he noticed the city's glow from behind the glass. The sun had gone down while he'd been asleep.

He crossed the room and pulled his phone from his bag. He entered the passcode and the phone lit up. It was just before eight in the evening. He'd been asleep for nearly two hours. An icon flashed, showing the receipt of two text messages. The first was a message from the Nepalese mobile network detailing the costs of using his phone. In Summary: loads. The second message was from Stockwell, demanding to know if he'd arrived and had made any progress. Leo put the phone down. He would reply later, probably.

Leo planned to spend the evening reviewing all his research on Allissa and her family.

He took out the photos and laid them across the bed, examining each one carefully. He wanted to try and think of Allissa as a friend. He didn't know why, possibly just a streak of unusual optimism, but somehow, he thought she was close. Leo knew Allissa could have left the city, got on any one of the buses that pulled out into the mountains every day. But then why would she need all that money?

Laying the final two photos on the bed cover, Leo stepped back and gazed down at the the assembled photographs. All the information he had on the Stockwells told of a hardworking, well-educated and wealthy family. Other than what Leo already knew about Blake Stockwell, the family seemed completely devoid of argument, incident, or public embarrassment. Almost too devoid of it. It was as though their reputation had been carefully stage-managed.

Leo scanned the pictures for anything hinting to a different story. It was interesting how, compared with the other Stockwell children, Allissa wasn't photographed often at all. Leo picked up one of the photographs. Stockwell presented a trophy to a small man in a jockey's outfit. Behind them, a glossy-coated horse looked dazed. Archie and Lucy stood at their father's feet. They were young children and grinned up at the camera. Leo guessed that Archie must have been around eight in the picture, meaning Lucy was around five, and Allissa two or three. But why wasn't Allissa there?

He replaced the photo and scanned the collection again. His eyes came to rest on a family photo which included Allissa. It looked as though it had been taken quite recently. The five members of the family stood in a well-manicured garden, most likely their Berkshire family home. Lord and Lady Stockwell stood in the center and the three children to the sides. Archie was on the right, Lucy and Allissa to the left. Lucy and Archie both had clear family resemblance; the reddened face, thick-set bodies and deep, intense eyes. Allissa was different. She didn't wear the contrived smiles of the others and glanced off to the right of the photographer. She was slender, dark-skinned, and her face was lit with a naturally bright expression. Her hair curled, loose and large, hinting at an African heritage. The only logical explanation, Leo supposed, tapping the edge of the picture, was that she had a different mother.

Before leaving, Leo had spent an evening trying to find out who Allissa's mother was. There was scant public information about Allissa Stockwell as it was, let alone her mother. Allissa had just appeared in the family around twenty years ago. Of course, it might be a coincidence, with a perfectly reasonable and logical explanation, but Leo doubted it. There was a mystery here and instinct told Leo that Blake Stockwell wanted it to stay that way.

Leo looked at the picture again. The way Allissa gazed absently off-camera made it look as though she wanted to be somewhere else. Without knowing why, Leo thought of his own family. He remembered a meal they'd shared two weeks ago, a time when he still had a job and knew nothing of Allissa, Lord Stockwell or Kathmandu. Surrounded by the coos and squeals of his two-year-old nephew, Leo had listened to talk of his sister and her husband's new house, how he should get a place of his own, and how they thought that still looking for Mya was a waste of time.

At that moment Leo felt as if he were the one looking out of the photograph. Physically he was there. Yet, he wanted to be somewhere else.

IN THE RESTAURANT, two men prepared for the evening's service. Their tiny dining room would be as busy as it always was. Customers would arrive, following the directions of someone who knew someone, all wanting to try the Himalayan Lamb. The restaurant was talked about as part of Kathmandu legend.

During the day, the restaurant was invisible without the hanging bulb illuminating the way. That's the way the men needed it to be. They were hiding in plain sight.

In the restaurant's kitchen, buried deep within the building, the men carefully prepared the meat. Sharp knives glinted as they sliced skin from flesh, flesh from bone. Foreheads prickled with perspiration as ovens were lit, and spices were added. Each man knew that preparation was key. The cut, the spice, the heat.

The phone on the wall of the kitchen rang. One of the men put down the knife and went to answer it. He picked up the receiver with bloodstained fingers.

The voice on the other end sounded distant. It was the call they had been expecting. They had a special job to do in the next day or so.

13

Allissa opened her eyes and took her first waking breath of the muggy morning air. She knew the day would be special. It was the day that everything would come together and fall in to place. The day the planets aligned, and things worked out to make her dream come true.

When Allissa had arrived in Kathmandu a few months before, she had known nothing of the plight of women like Chimini and Fuli. Women who had been lied to, imprisoned and abused, all for the pleasure of cruel and greedy men. She'd just been moving around the world with no real plan. No purpose. Just to see, and to experience. To not go home.

In those early Kathmandu days, Allissa wandered the dusty streets, seeing little to separate the manic city from many others across Asia. Sure, it had nice sites — temples, bazaars and the surrounding mountains — but there had been nothing to persuade her to stay. On what was supposed to be her final day, Allissa met a group of charity workers in a restaurant. The place was busy, and they invited her to join their table. They spoke of countries they'd visited, and adventures they'd had — in the way backpackers do wherever they meet the world over. Then one young lady had told Allissa of the work they did.

They visited remote villages high in the mountains, days from anywhere else, in order to spread the word about the gangs of men who also made the same journeys. Gangs who promised the village's young women jobs in the big city. Jobs which, when they arrived in the city, were nothing more than time spent on a soiled mattress in a dark room.

With the restaurant bustling around them, listening to tales of the work the team were doing, Allissa realized she'd been doing it all wrong. She'd been traveling the world looking for something she needed. Searching for something she felt was missing. What she needed in fact, was to find a way in which the world needed her. In the people around that table, all those months ago, Allissa started to find it.

The conversations continued late into the night,

and enthralled Allissa so much that she asked if she could join them on their next trip. She left Kathmandu two days later, along with three others: Kate, a young man from Canada, and a Nepalese girl called Chimini. For a month they'd journeyed to some of the remotest parts of the country, visiting some of the poorest and most undeveloped villages. By the time they returned to Kathmandu, Allissa knew what she was going to do. Her dream had been formed. It was a dream which, with the arrival of the furniture for the guesthouse today, would finally be complete.

Leo winced as he stepped out into the street. The traffic growled past, kicking up dust and filling the air with fumes. Leo eyes stung and his lungs burned, but that was a feeling he would have to get used to. He would be in Kathmandu for a few days, maybe even weeks.

Leo waved at an approaching taxi. Learning from his experience of two days ago, Leo handed the driver a piece of paper which detailed the destination he required. He had a small stack of The Best Kathmandu Guesthouse's business cards for the return journey.

Ten minutes later, the taxi stopped outside the SNC Everest Bank. Leo paid the driver, got out and looked up at the bank's front door. It didn't look like the sort of place from which you could withdraw a small fortune. It didn't really look like they knew anything about money at all.

Like many of the businesses in Kathmandu, the bank occupied one unit on the ground floor of a four-storey concrete building. Except for the faded red and green sign, it was indistinguishable from the shops on either side. Sun-bleached posters taped to the inside of the glass advertized the services the bank offered: *ATM, International Money Transfer, and Safety Deposit Boxes.*

Leo took a deep breath, tried to ignore his rising anxiety, and stepped inside.

The bank itself was nothing more than a small room, gloomy in comparison to the harsh, muggy daylight. Dust streaked across the floor and a faded ATM blinked from the shadows. A Nepalese lady spoke harshly on the phone behind the desk in the corner.

Leo approached the desk. The bank teller continued her conversation for several minutes before putting the phone down. Finally, she spoke to Leo in Nepalese. Leo couldn't even decipher where one word ended and the next began, let alone understand their meaning.

"Do you speak English?" Leo asked hopefully. "I'm looking for my sister."

Leo had decided that his best option was to pretend to be Allissa's brother. That way, his interest in her was easily explained. Perhaps people would even feel sorry for him.

The teller looked up at him, her expression blank.

"She visited this bank," Leo said, he slipped out the picture of Allissa and showed it to the teller. She peered carefully at the picture.

For a fraction of a second, Leo thought he saw a flicker of recognition. Allissa was the sort of person someone would remember.

The lady spoke in Nepalese again.

"I don't understand," Leo said, his palms out in surrender. "I'm sorry."

"Manu," the lady shouted.

Leo straightened up.

"Manu," she shouted again.

There was no response. Leo looked nervously around the bank.

The woman stood walked to the doorway at the rear of the bank. She pulled aside a curtain and shouted through. "Manu! Manu!"

Kathmandu Killers

A distant male voice replied, followed by the sound of movement.

Leo turned and checked the door behind him, as though making sure he could run away if he needed to. Traffic thudded past continuously, shaking the door in its frame.

"Hello, can I help?" said a man as he pushed through the curtain and strode into the room. "My wife said" — he indicated the woman behind the desk with a wave — "you are looking for someone. How can I help?"

"Yes," Leo said. "My sister. I have a picture. She withdrew some money here two weeks ago."

The man leaned over and peered at the photo. Leo again watched for any sign of recognition. This time he saw none.

The man turned and spoke to the woman for some time.

Leo watched the exchange, his head whipping from side to side like a tennis spectator.

Eventually the man turned back to Leo. "My wife says that, yes, your sister was here. My wife did not think we should tell you that, but I do not see the harm. I am sorry to say we cannot tell you any more."

"I'll pay," Leo said, pulling out a small bundle of

notes. "If you can tell me the address my sister gave you, I'll pay."

The woman interjected with a torrent of words, pointing at the money. Leo couldn't tell whether she was excited or insulted.

"No," the man said, pointing at the door. "We have a responsibility of secrecy to our clients. I have already said too much."

A rock formed in Leo's throat. He glanced at the door. To leave now would be to leave with nothing.

"Please." Leo knitted his fingers together and took a step forward. "You have to help me. My sister's in Kathmandu all alone. We're all worried about her. We've not seen or heard from her in years."

The man's arms dropped to his side. He looked from his wife to Leo and back again.

"I need to know where she is," Leo said, his pulse raging.

The man shifted his weight from one foot to the other.

"I'm sorry," he said.

"Do you have any children yourself?" Leo stepped to the side so that he could address both the man and the woman. "Imagine if they were lost on the other side of the world."

The man spoke to his wife, she replied sharply as though shutting down his protests.

"I'm sorry," the man said, looking at the floor. "We cannot tell you anything about our customers. I wish you luck in finding your sister, but I can't do any more to help you."

"Please, you have to," Leo said, glancing from one stony face to the other.

The door swung open and a short woman bustled into the bank. Exhaust fumes and dust filled the room.

"No," the man said. "We have customers now, so you have to go." He pointed at the door. "I wish you luck and sorry we cannot help."

Leo sighed, that had been his only lead. Reluctantly, he stepped out into the dazzling sunlight with nothing.

14

Back in his hotel room, Leo ran over the events of the afternoon. He'd done everything he could to get the address from the man and woman in the bank. He supposed if he really were Allissa's brother, knowing that she was alive and well would be reassuring. For him, though, that wasn't enough.

Leo blinked. He'd spent the last two hours researching on his laptop via the hotel's frustrating Wi-Fi. His eyes and neck ached. On the pad in front of him he'd scrawled the addresses of hotels and guest-houses close to the bank. They would be his first stops tomorrow. Leo also needed to find someone who spoke Nepalese to help him.

Leo's stomach rumbled. He'd hardly eaten in the last few days. He put the laptop on the bed and stretched, then crossed to the window. He hadn't even noticed the light fade.

The weather had deteriorated throughout the afternoon. By the time Leo's taxi had cut through the busy streets on the way back to the hotel, burgeoning dark clouds had thickened on all sides. Moisture in the air promised rain that so far hadn't arrived. Beyond the window, the turbulent sky brooded. It matched Leo's mood.

Leo glanced down and noticed there was a restaurant just beside the guesthouse. Strings of Chinese lanterns hung above the outdoor dining area. Giving in to his grumbling stomach, Leo left his room and walked down the stairs. Two minutes later, he crossed to an empty table at the back of the restaurant.

Sliding into one of the four chairs, Leo glanced around. The casual noise of conversation was calming, as was the idea that he didn't need to be part of it. Solitude was good.

"Don't eat too much," said a lady with a New York accent from the next table. "I wanna go to that restaurant later."

"Well yeah, but we might not find it, and I'm hungry now," replied the man opposite her, tearing into a flatbread.

Leo flicked through the menu. Many dishes were clearly named for the benefit of tourists: Sherpa Chicken, Gurkha Chulo, Everest Stew.

As Leo was trying and struggling to decode one of the menu's awkwardly translated descriptions, a beer appeared on the table.

"When in Rome," Leo muttered to himself. He picked up the bottle and took a sip. Leo called one of the waiters over and ordered a range of dishes. It would definitely be too much food, but it was cheap, and he was hungry.

Far above the hanging lanterns, the first flash lightning rippled across the sky. Right now, it was far enough away to be over the mountains, but there was no doubt it would come. Leo sipped at the cold beer and wondered about the rain. It was raining in Brighton when he'd left, and now electricity in the air promised the same. Leo knew the story of God flooding the world in punishment. On an international scale that seemed impossible. On a personal level, he was less confident. Maybe Leo had upset the Almighty and was now his target the world over.

"Hey, you mind if we join you?" A female voice punctured his daydream. Leo looked up at the voice's owner. She was short and skinny, with aggressive red hair and an American accent.

"Sure, of course," Leo said before he knew what he was saying.

The newcomer waved her friends over. "I'm Jem, this is Katelyn, and this is Tau," the girl said, pointing out her friends as they crossed the restaurant. Leo introduced himself.

"Thanks for that, mate," said Tau, the last to sit down opposite Leo. "Really didn't fancy going back out on the street looking for somewhere else. Just need to eat!" He reached over and picked up the menu.

"You had lunch not that long ago," teased Jem.

"Yeah, like two hours or something," Tau replied. "I'm a growing lad." He rubbed his stomach, then frowned as he tried to make sense of the menu.

"Have you been here before?" Leo asked.

"We've only just arrived," Tau said, looking at him over the top of the menu. "Came over on the bus from Pokhara today. It's one of my favorite journeys, but it's so long."

"Yeah, I swear that driver was pissed," said Jem. "We were wobbling about all over the place."

"What's it like?" Leo asked. "In Pokhara, I mean."

"It's great," said Tau. "Very cool city. Lakes and

mountains. Loads of places to eat and drink. What are you drinking here?" Tau picked up Leo's beer. "How is it?"

Jem and Kaitlyn fell into conversation across the table.

"Just ordered a beer," Leo said, omitting the fact he hadn't ordered it at all. "Wasn't sure what the local one was, but it seems alright."

"Yeah right, the local ones are pretty good. Some are even better than our Indian ones. Gurkha's been the best I've had." Tau turned the bottle in his hands. "Ahh, Everest. This is decent too." Tau extended a broad arm in the air and shouted a few words in Nepalese.

"You speak Nepalese," Leo said, suddenly interested.

"I know a few words," Tau replied.

"Rubbish, you know more than a few words," said Jen. "He's got us everything we need in the last few days."

"You come from Nepal?"

"My family live in Varanasi, northern India, but I've been coming here for years. It's just a great place to, you know, relax."

Leo nodded, understanding Tau's meaning. "Where had you been before Pokhara?"

"Two-week trip from Delhi," Jem said. "All overland, a lot of buses and trains. Just happened to bump into this guy on the way." Jem pointed at Tau. "But tonight, it ends."

The waiter slid the beers onto the table.

"Tomorrow, we go our separate ways," Tau said. "Well, these two do. I'm around for a couple more days. How about you?"

"I'm..." Leo mumbled, not knowing what to say. He didn't know how to explain his task here without sounding like a fraud. He wasn't a detective. He was just a guy who knew a little bit about finding people because of some bad luck.

"Well, it's a bit of a long story..." Leo said, pausing, waiting for a distraction or a change of topic. Tau encouraged him with a flick of the bottle. Leo sighed. "I'm basically here to find a missing person."

Tau's eyes widened. "That's so cool," he said. "Who?"

Leo explained about Allissa, about Blake Stockwell, about the website.

Tau, Kaitlyn, and Jem gasped at Stockwell's out-of-the-blue arrival and brimmed with excitement when Leo said that had accepted the challenge.

"How did you start out looking for missing people then?" asked Jem.

Leo took a long, restorative sip of his beer. Leo glanced at the people around the table. He'd known them for less than thirty minutes, but he was already opening up to them. At home, he didn't talk about Mya, the website, or his hopes of finding her. People seemed to treat him differently once they found out. On the other side of the world, though, in the warm company of strangers, there seemed to be none of that judgement.

Drawing a deep breath, Leo began to explain.

15

Four months before Mya's disappearance. Brighton, England.

"I've got it all planned," Mya said as Leo walked into the front room. The afternoon light poured through streaky windows and lay in angular patches on the floor. The somber shriek of seagulls was still audible through the thin glass.

"We needed to go for two months though," she said, looking toward him, judging his reaction.

"I thought we said one month?" Leo replied.

"We did, at first, yeah, but then I looked at this." She pointed at the map stretched out on the floor. "By the time we had paid for the flights, we might as well stay the extra month. Come here. I'll show you."

After a long, tiring week at the newspaper, Leo wanted nothing more than to sit still and close his eyes.

"It's literally the trip I've always wanted," Mya said, beckoning him to come. Leo smiled reluctantly and crossed the room. Mya traced their proposed journey with a delicate finger.

"We'll go to Mumbai first," she said. "That's on the west coast of India. It's the capital city — a real introduction into Asia. We'll go and visit the real slums and everything, see the people who live there..."

Leo sat on the sofa and watched Mya. She glanced up at him and he nodded obediently. He wanted to please her so much. He wanted to. But he just couldn't.

How could he tell her two months was impossible? Getting the editor to agree to one had been hard enough. The problem was, with the recent takeover of the paper, staff leaving, things changing, they couldn't do without him. The only way he had even been able to get one month off was by promising to check-in online every couple of days, though he hadn't told Mya that yet.

"But you deserve the time off," was her usual retort. "They don't care about you. They're wasting your time."

And the hardest thing was, Leo partly agreed.

Maybe he was wasting his time. But he didn't know what else to do.

"Then for the second month," Mya continued, turning to look at him. Leo's smile thawed in frustration. "... we'll fly over to Bangkok..."

Then, there was the decision he'd made. The biggest ever. A decision so big, he would need a job to see it through. Weddings were expensive.

KATHMANDU, **Nepal. Present Day.**

IN THE RESTAURANT with the Chinese lanterns, Tau, Jem and Kaitlyn listened in silence as Leo told of Mya's disappearance.

"I almost wasn't going to come," Leo said. "I don't know anything about finding people in the real world, but I thought, what would Mya want me to do? So, I came to look for this girl. Sounds pretty unbelievable, doesn't it?"

Three silent stares followed from the others around the table. It felt strange for Leo to be this honest with people he hardly knew. He was enjoying it.

"Wow, man, that's awesome," Tau said. "Some old millionaire has basically paid you to come on holiday to try and find his daughter?"

"Yeah, I guess. Though it's not really been a holiday so far," Leo added, straightening with pride.

"That's so sad about your girlfriend, though," said Jem. "That must've been awful."

"Yeah, it was." Leo nodded. "I've had no luck finding her. She's not been seen anywhere in two years."

"Man, that's so hard," said Kaitlyn, shaking her head. "I wouldn't even know where to start looking, nor what to do."

"Well, that's the thing, most people don't. There's no clear way even to start, particularly when it's in a different country and they're adults. That's why I set the site up."

The other three nodded.

"So, you're like some kind of detective now," Tau said.

"How are you going to find her?" Jem asked.

"I'd done a fair bit of research before leaving England and started to trace her today. I know where she's been. Now I just need to work out where she is."

"What do you need to do next?" Jem asked.

"Bit of an obvious one. Find someone who speaks

Kathmandu Killers

English and Nepalese. Even finding a hotel around here is hard enough without knowing the language."

Everyone looked at Tau and an awkward silence descended over the table.

"Well, I know where you need to start looking tonight," Tau said, banging the tabletop. "Torro's bar!"

Jem and Kaitlyn rolled their eyes in unison.

"I'm just saying that if this Allissa will be anywhere tonight, she'll be at Torro's bar. That's where the party is every night in this city."

"This guy does know all the parties," Jem said. "That's the sort of person you need to know."

Leo glanced at Tau. Tau seemed like an outgoing guy who knew the local area and who could speak the language, which was exactly what Leo needed. Looking around at the others, Leo dared to let a feeling of positivity rise inside him.

"Where is this place then," Leo said.

"I'll show you," Tau said. "We're celebrating. Our last night and everything."

Jem explained that she was moving on, down towards Southeast Asia. Kaitlyn was going home, back to Cambridge in England. She glowed when she mentioned her boyfriend collecting her from the airport. She made it sound like the trip away had been challenging.

Tau took a packet of cigarettes from his jeans and offered them around the table. Leo and Kaitlyn shook their heads, Jem took one.

"Let's get some food then," Tau said. "Then head over to this bar. It's the place to be. Come with us Leo. You never know, your missing woman might just be there."

Leo had planned to go back to his hotel and get some rest ahead of a productive day tomorrow, but checking out this bar and getting Tau to agree to help would be a breakthrough.

"Yeah, you totally should," Jem said. "You'd enjoy it. You never know what you might find." She laughed upwards, exhaling smoke.

"I'm not going to be out late though guys. I've got a long flight tomorrow," said Kaitlyn, looking over her shoulder at a passing waiter.

Jem and Tau rolled their eyes.

More beers arrived, followed by bowl upon bowl of creamy, luscious fresh curries, rice, and baskets of buttery naan bread.

"Most of the food here is vegetables," Tau said. "There are loads of vegetarians because of their religions, but also because meat is really hard to get here."

He shoved a rolled-up flatbread into one of the bowls for the second time and scooped it into his

Kathmandu Killers 93

mouth. Kaitlyn looked disapprovingly. Leo was getting the impression they didn't mind if she left early.

"I don't eat meat anyway," Kaitlyn said, carefully scooping one of the creamiest curries onto her rice.

"Ahh, you're missing out," Tau said, grinning. "The meat can be touch and go if you don't know where to get it. You see the scraggy little chickens kept in cages on the street. There's nothing to them. Not like the corn-fed fat ones they serve in the good places."

"This is pretty good though," Jem said, finishing off one of the bowls. "Feels like we've not eaten in ages."

"You haven't. It's been like two hours," said Tau. "This girl can certainly eat!" He flicked Jem a smile, and she kicked him under the table.

A group of young Nepalese men at the table behind Tau finished their drinks and made off laughing into the night. The couple by the door ate slowly, deep in conversation. A large, plainly dressed man sat in the far corner. He drank a beer and looked up from his phone to the restaurant and back again. He was at odds with the upbeat mood of the restaurant.

Watching the others demolish the food, Leo felt an unwelcome stampede of jealousy. It was as though they had a freedom he'd lost. Jem and Tau had clearly become close in the last two weeks. Leo knew how they'd feel when Jem had to leave in the morning.

When Leo and Mya were traveling, they'd stayed up late, got up early, and squeezed as much as possible into each and every day. Mya wanted to do everything unless it was stupid and dangerous, then she really wanted to do it. At the time, Leo often thought they were lucky to survive uninjured. Maybe if they'd been more careful things would have ended differently.

He knew he was going to have to do things that made him uncomfortable to find Allissa. Probably even things that were dangerous too.

Tau scraped the bowls with bread, then cleaned his fingers on a napkin.

"Right, let's go," he said.

"I'm going back to the hotel," Kaitlyn said, pausing Tau's rise from the chair. Tau and Jem made a convincing attempt to dissuade her, and Leo chipped in with some friendly encouragement. "It's been a long day, and that bus has pretty much done me in," Kaitlyn said, dismissing their efforts to change her mind.

"Let us walk you back," Jem said.

"No, honestly, I'll be fine. The hotel is only there. Thank you, though." Kaitlyn stood, gave some money to Jem for the food, and walked away.

Two miles away, Allissa, Chimini and Fuli rushed in and out of the guesthouse's seven rooms. Together they made beds, folded towels, swept floors and busied themselves with the finishing touches.

By the time the work was complete and the three sat together around the small kitchen table, the night's darkness had long since descended.

To Allissa and Chimini, the guesthouse represented months of hard work. Months of calculating finances, finding the location, agreeing on a deal with the owner, and now setting up the rooms for the guests. To Fuli, it represented a future. A new start, from which she could build a life for herself.

"I bought something for us, for this night," Allissa said, standing and crossing to the fridge. The girls watched as she removed a bottle.

"What is it?" Chimini asked.

"Champagne," Allissa said. The girls looked at her blankly. "It's a fizzy wine we have in England when we're celebrating something. You do *not* want to know how much it cost."

"Fizzy wine?" Chimini repeated.

"You wait 'til you try some," Allissa said. "You'll love it."

Allissa placed the bottle in the middle of the table, then pulled three mugs of different colors and sizes from a cupboard. They definitely weren't the crystal flutes which adorned the tables at Stockwell Manor, but they would do the job.

"This might make a bit of noise," Allissa said, removing the wire cage. Chimini warned Fuli, whose grin hadn't dropped all evening.

The girls looked excitedly from one to another as the cork popped in Allissa's steady hands, and a tiny stream of bubbles ran down the stem of the bottle.

"Now we have to do this." Allissa poured champagne into each of the cups and pushed them across the table. "Hold them up like this."

Allissa looked at the two young women. It was a moment she knew she wanted to remember. "To the future." Allissa's eyes moistened at their beaming smiles as she took her first sip.

16

The street outside the restaurant with the Chinese lanterns was quiet. The traffic had subsided to the occasional taxi, which stormed past in a hail of dust and grit.

Even in the day, Kathmandu wasn't easy to navigate. At night, when the only light seeped from windows and passing cars, it was virtually impossible. Each street wound organically from the next, as though it had grown that way over centuries. As Tau, Jem and Leo groped their way through the puddles of light and darkness, Leo reminded himself to make sure he left with the others.

After fifteen minutes they approached a man standing alone in the street. He was the first person they'd come across on the whole journey.

"This is it." Tau pointed at the man.

Leo glanced up at the glowing windows which seemed to hover against the sky.

"This is the sort of place you'd never find without knowing it was there," Tau said.

The solitary man opened a door between the locked shutters of two shops. Music thudded into the street.

"This place has been going for years." Tau's voice got louder to counter the music. "Torro's the guy who owns it."

Tau pushed open a second door and stepped inside. Leo winced at the smell of beer, cigarettes, and the loud thump of rock music. People around the room sipped from drinks and stamped to the beat.

"First things first, let's get a beer," Tau said. "You gotta meet Torro!"

Leo scanned the room as Tau led them toward the bar. It would be incredible just to see Allissa here. He looked from one group of people to the next, but none matched her description.

Tau pushed towards the bar, waved a note above his head and shouted over the noise of the music.

"Man, that night was so good…"

Leo could only hear fragments of their conversations.

Kathmandu Killers

"I'm going to remember that forever…"

"Your face was incredible…"

Tau was acting out some part of the remembered night when the barman approached. He recognized Tau, offered a handshake, but didn't smile.

"Guys, this is Torro," Tau said.

Torro shook hands with everyone as Tau ordered drinks. Torro was a big man, wide and tall. He had long hair and one half of his mouth slanted downwards, giving him a constant frown.

"Torro doesn't speak English," Tau explained. "He's lived in Kathmandu for over forty years. He's one of the originals. In the seventies, this was one of the destinations for the Hippy Trail across Asia. Loads of people used to come here and just get lost for weeks. That great man! Torro's one of those, but just never left."

Torro returned with three beers in one hand and four shot glasses in the other. The beers were distributed as Torro poured out the shots.

"The first one to swallow pays," Tau said, pouring the shot into his mouth and washing it around his teeth. Torro did the same, his sharp eyes following the other three.

The chemical taste of alcohol burned Leo's mouth. Leo had never been a big drinker. He'd taken shots before but never particularly enjoyed them. Leo watched the others, copying their swilling of the rancid drink. The liquid tasted like acid.

"Urrrrgggh!" Tau shouted, pouring beer into his mouth. Jem did the same.

"Ahhhh, drinks on you!" Jem said, slapping Tau on the back.

Leaning against the bar, Leo noticed that the walls of the room were covered with dozens of small, yellowing photographs. Each was a tiny portrait; the type used for passports or visa applications. Leo did a three sixty turn. Hundreds of photos covered every available space. Leo wondered whether these people ever thought about their picture on the wall of Torro's Bar.

"You got any plans the next couple of days," Leo said to Tau.

"Just ask me if you need help man, it sounds fun!"

Leo grinned. "Do you fancy helping an almost down and out detective find a missing person?"

Tau held up his empty beer bottle. "Replace this for me, and you've got a deal."

"Sounds good to me." Leo bought another round for the three of them.

"What do you know about this chick, then?" Tau said, taking a sip from the fresh bottle.

Kathmandu Killers

"There's something interesting about her family. She's got a half-brother and a sister. I believe she feels a bit like the odd one out. That may have something to do with this."

"Was she traveling alone?"

"As far as I know, yes. She left on her own, but she's been away for two years now, so she could be with anyone."

"Okay," Tau said decisively. "What's your feeling? Is she in the city or has she moved on?"

"I'm not sure, but I'm going to assume she's still here until I learn otherwise."

Tau paused, running through places in his mind. "That gives us a few options. Let's talk in more detail tomorrow and make a plan."

The door swung open and another group of people jostled into the bar, sweaty bodies moving to the beat of the music. The bar was now far beyond comfortably busy.

One song faded and the next began — *'London Calling'*, by The Clash.

"We're gonna shoot off now, Jem's last night an all," Tau said, shouting over the music. "Do you wanna walk back with us?"

Leo agreed, finished his beer, and they fought their way towards the door. They shoved through the doors and stepped out onto the street. Leo took a deep breath, although the air out here was cooler, it still wasn't refreshing. The traffic had dwindled but the smell of choking exhaust still lingered.

Jem clattered through the door, a cigarette already hanging from her lips. "Let's go," she said, lighting up and then turning towards Tau. "We're on the clock tonight."

Tau put his arm on the base of Jem's back and kissed her on the neck.

Seeing their affection, Leo thought of the photos on the walls of the bar. Those photos were the faded ghosts of good times in the past. For Tau, that's what Jem would be tomorrow. Just a memory. Leo knew a thing or two about memories. He knew that, however much you wanted them to stay fresh in your mind, like the pictures on the walls of the bar, they would fade with age.

That's the way memories worked. They were the past, and once something was in the past, you could never get it back, however much you wanted it.

17

Five weeks until Mya's disappearance. Mumbai to Delhi train, India.

"This will help us sleep," Mya said, crumbling a bud of dried cannabis over two papers, skillfully compensating for the rocking of the train. They were traveling north from Mumbai to Delhi, nearly halfway through the nineteen-hour journey.

The train moved slowly, rumbling its way through fields where people ambled home after their day's work. Wisps of smoke curled upwards from houses of rusty corrugated metal.

First licking, then rolling the spliff tight, Mya tucked it behind her ear and jumped from the bunk in the second-class sleeping section. Leo followed her to the toilet cubicle at the end of the carriage. They passed families bedding down for the night, children in colorful pajamas, and older people playing cards.

Cramming into the cubicle, they closed the door and stood over the hole in the floor used as a toilet. Mya lit up, and the spliff flared to life. She took the first inhalation, held it for a moment, and let the thick smoke go. It danced across the inches that separated them before streaming through the small barred window.

A violent hand knocked at the door, followed by barked instructions in Hindi.

"They'll go away," Mya said, taking another pull.

The hand knocked again. The same barked instructions.

A key grated in the lock and the door opened. The train guard stood there. His gaze swung from Mya to Leo, then down to the lit spliff between Mya's fingers. There was no getting away with it.

"You cannot smoke in here," the guard said.

"Where can we smoke then?" Mya replied cheekily.

The guard beckoned them to follow and pulled open the train's door. Fields sprawled toward the horizon, beyond which the sun made its final descent. The guard pointed to the step on the outside of the train.

Mya sat down, and Leo followed.

The guard pushed the door, almost closing it behind them.

The rails slid sedately below their hanging feet. The train's horn bellowed as they clattered into a corner.

Leo gazed out at the countryside, big leaved trees, red earthen paths, fresh shoots of crops above square-cut fields all slowly sinking into shadow. The pinks of the sinking sun were mirrored hundreds of times in corrugated metal roofs and patches of water, making a patchwork of light and dark beneath the cloud-speckled sky.

Leo looked at Mya, her face pink in the dying daylight.

Now would be a good time to ask, Leo knew. Now would be an unforgettable time. They would never be there again.

But, the ring was in his bag back at their bunks. He could have done it, regardless. The moment was perfect. Leo inhaled; the wet air smelled like vegetation.

"I love how you never know what's going to happen," Mya said, breaking the silence and handing Leo the spliff. "I always want to keep exploring."

Leo knew she was right; that's why the moment needed to be perfect. He had one chance to get it right.

Mya slid closer as Leo took a drag. The train rumbled around another curve and left the moment behind.

Present day. Kathmandu.

The restaurant was busy. Customers continued to find their way to the door identified only by the bare bulb.

Look for the light. You've got to look for the light.

The restaurant had never been advertised and the location wasn't officially known. Yet somehow, the legend of the Himalayan Lamb passed from tourist to tourist in the hostels and bars of The Mountain City.

Over the years, the restaurant had received much critical acclaim, once making it into a guidebook. *"You have not been to Kathmandu unless you've eaten there,"* the listing said, giving vague directions about how to find it in the warren of crisscrossing passages.

In truth, it would be impossible to find during the day, or when the bulb was not illuminated, which added to the elusive excitement backpackers lapped up.

18

Storms rolled around Kathmandu during the night, but none managed to break into the city. Sooner or later, they would crack the anticipation which hung thick and heavy in the air.

Leo lay awake in his hotel room, listening to thunder crash and tumble. He hoped no one would be hurt on the mountain passes as the storms pushed through the valleys.

After getting back from the bar, he'd showered, changed and gone to bed. He hadn't realized how much he'd drank until he lay down. The walls seemed to move and sway with his thoughts, and the ceiling fan rattled at such a volume that Leo wondered whether anyone in the building was asleep.

With growing frustration, Leo tried to work out

what time it would be in Brighton right now. After several minutes he gave up, the concept of time and travel tied him in cognitive knots. As usual, all he ended up thinking about, was Mya.

He was angry, sad, and tired. At her, at himself, at being in this hotel on his own in a strange city, at Torro's unusual citrus shot that he could still taste on his breath, at the world for taking away things that were good and pure and honest, and at the fact that he hadn't had a proper night's sleep in nearly two days.

Finally, the tiredness took over and Leo succumbed to a disturbed and restless sleep, much like the city outside.

Leo awoke after what seemed like a heartbeat. Light piled in through the half-open curtains, dazzling him as his eyes struggled to adjust. He searched without movement for any injuries, and scanned the final memories of the night before. He wasn't used to drinking that much.

Confident that he'd remembered everything, sure he wasn't hurt, and certain he was in his hotel room, Leo finally sat up.

Leo and Tau swapped phone numbers last night and Leo hoped they'd be able to get started this morning. Perhaps, with the way he felt now, it would be better to wait until the afternoon.

He reached for his phone on the bedside table. Two texts.

The first from Stockwell: *You're in Kathmandu now. I expect to hear news soon.*

The second from Tau: *Dude, I'll be at your hotel in thirty minutes.*

Leo checked the time the message had been sent, twelve-thirty. Twenty minutes ago.

Leo sighed. How had Tau managed that? The guy must be a machine.

Fifteen minutes later, Leo scuttled down the stairs to the hotel lobby. Finding Tau was a step forward in the investigation, Leo didn't want to keep him waiting.

As Leo ran into the lobby, Tau rose from one of the bedraggled sofas on the far side of the gloomy space. He wore dark leather shoes, blue faded jeans and a baggy t-shirt with a logo Leo didn't recognize. His clothing and manner seemed to bridge both the city they were in, and the world Leo knew. Leo found it reassuring.

"Jem get off okay?" Leo said.

"Sure," Tau said, shrugging a gesture that meant far more than the words spoken. "How'd you like Torro's then?" Tau asked.

"It was fine while I was there... when I got back here was the problem."

"Yeah, you look like you're in trouble, dude!" Tau said.

Leo shook his head slowly.

"Let's get some coffee, then we'll make a plan," Tau suggested. "Have you brought the stuff you have on this girl?" Tau nodded toward Leo's empty hands.

A few minutes later Leo returned with the folder of information he had collected on Allissa and the Stockwell family. Tau was waiting by the door, smoking a cigarette.

Leo joined Tau on the street. The city this morning looked especially bright and chaotic. Leo followed Tau as they set off down the road. He had to concentrate to walk side by side in the gap between the buildings and the traffic. Rubbish, abandoned vehicles and drainage ditches all lay ready to cause a fall or break an ankle. Twice they even had to dodge goats tied to the side of the buildings.

Tau chose a café, and they sat at the table in the window. The place was air-conditioned and quiet.

"I reckon you need to eat," Tau said, flicking Leo a menu.

Tau ordered eggs and Leo tried to explain to the waitress the phenomenon of cheese on toast. Tau was already coming into his own, offering some words of translation that the waitress hadn't understood. They both ordered large coffees. Nepali coffee, Tau explained, was served dark and bitter, and without milk.

The coffee arrived quickly, followed minutes later by the food. The sight of Tau's eggs made Leo even more hungry. This cheese on toast was going to be good. By the time the waitress slammed a plate down in front of Leo, he was so ready for it. Looking at the plate, his heart sank. Two bits of cold toast and a block of pale cheese sat beside each other on the plate. Leo exhaled the disappointment. Today was going to be challenging, he could tell.

When the caffeine had started to do its work, Leo and Tau turned to the business at hand.

"Show me what we've got," Tau said, rubbing his hands together.

Leo opened the folder and produced one of the photos.

"Allissa Stockwell," he said, passing the picture to Tau.

"She's a pretty girl," Tau said, reaching out for the photo and examining it closely.

"She is," Leo agreed. "It was her father, Blake Stockwell, a politician, who asked me to find her." He passed over the photo of the Stockwell family. "She's Stockwell's daughter, but to a different mother than his other two children, I think. There's nothing known about who her mother is, or at least if there is I can't find it. Allissa just seems to appear in the family when she's about five. She keeps a low profile generally but was brought up in the same way as the others."

Tau placed the photo down in line with the other on the table.

"How old is she now?"

"Just turned twenty-eight a few weeks ago."

"What's her story then?"

Leo ran through what he knew about Allissa. "They were expecting her to follow her mother — her stepmother, I suppose — into law. Then one day she just disappears. No word to the family or anything. Just disappears. A few weeks later she contacts them to say she's gone traveling. She's fine, doesn't know when she'll be back." Leo shivered as the air-conditioner's stream of cold air clipped the back of his neck.

"And she didn't come back?" Tau looked up from the photograph.

"They hadn't heard from her until a few weeks ago when she contacted her sister, Lucy. She asked Lucy to arrange the transfer of thirty-five-thousand dollars from a trust fund to an account she'd set up here." Leo paused to judge Tau's reaction at the amount of money. There was none. "Lucy said she'd do it, but she needed to know where Allissa was so that they could all stop worrying. They had a long phone conversation one evening, and Allissa said she was really happy."

"Did you speak to Lucy?" Tau asked.

"No, Stockwell told me this. He doesn't want anyone from the family to know he's sent me to look for her."

"That's a bit suspicious," Tau said. "How do we know she's in Kathmandu at all?"

"Stockwell found out the account number that the money had been sent to. He's a well-connected guy and managed to trace it to a bank here. I went there yesterday and pretended to be her brother. I showed the teller a picture of Allissa and the teller confirmed that Allissa had visited the bank. They wouldn't tell me the address she'd given, though. I even offered to pay them."

Tau's eyebrows twisted in concern. Through the window, a bulging lorry crawled past, almost scraping the front of the buildings.

"I don't think she would've withdrawn that money and left the city," Leo said. "I think she had a plan to spend it on something local. We work out what that is, we find her."

"Yes, *we* will," Tau said with emphasis, focusing his

stare on Leo. "You're definitely going to need my help on this, yes?"

Leo nodded.

"Well, this rich guy is obviously paying you for it, so I'll need a hundred dollars a day, plus you pay any expenses."

Leo wasn't going to argue. Finding Tau was a stroke of luck, and not one he was going to give up.

"Fine," he said, reaching across the table now strewn with papers and photos to shake Tau's hand.

"We need to go back to the bank," Tau said, his face opening into a smile. "If it's the sort of place I think it is, then I have an idea about how to get her address."

19

When Allissa emerged from her room that morning, Fuli and Chimini were already behind the reception desk talking in animated excitement.

"Hello, welcome to the Teku Guesthouse," Chimini said.

"Hello, welcome Teku Guessouse," Fuli repeated back. They'd kept the same name for the guesthouse as the previous occupants. Although they had considered changing it, for a fresh start, they weren't sure what to change it to, and there was already a sign outside advertising it.

Fuli and Chimini smiled as Allissa walked towards them.

"You will never guess what has happened," Chimini said.

"Welcome, Teku, Guessouse," Fuli repeated quietly.

"We have our first guest," Chimini said before Allissa could answer. "She checked in about an hour ago."

"Wow, that's brilliant," Allissa said. "All checked in okay?"

"Yes, yes, of course," Chimini said, looking down at the large logbook now with one row filled in. "Paid upfront for three nights, double room."

Allissa smiled at Chimini's excitement. The thing they'd wanted and worked so hard for many months to achieve had at last come together. It was there. It had happened. Turning toward the kitchen, away from the women at the reception desk, Allissa let the smile drain from her face.

"Welcome," Fuli began again.

Allissa closed the door of the kitchen behind her. She didn't know why she couldn't be as happy about the opening of the guesthouse as Fuli and Chimini. She wanted to be. Wanted it so much. Allissa thought that getting the guesthouse together would give her a purpose, a place where she was needed and a sense of belonging. So far, it hadn't.

Although she now knew a few Nepalese words, she

didn't speak the language, and the few streets she knew around the city didn't make it hers.

Allissa filled the kettle, clicked it on, and looked out into the thuggish morning. They were all alike — herself, Chimini, Fuli. They had all been through things which they carried around their necks — millstones against the world. Allissa had left England to clear her mind of the things she knew, yet the memories had followed her here.

Allissa rubbed her eyes with the heels of her hands as the kettle growled to a boil. She knew she would have to face him one day. She would have to deal with the issues that she held so close, the issues which had inspired her to help some of the most vulnerable people in the world. Rinsing the cups they'd drank champagne from the previous night and spooning instant coffee into one, Allissa thought that often it was with the same strength that you ran and remembered. The harder you ran, the stronger you became, the more vivid the surging memories.

Allissa realized then, that two years of running, covering thousands of miles, meant nothing when the millstone of her memories was with her the whole time.

ON THE SHORT taxi ride to the bank, Tau explained his plan. Leo was not convinced it would work but felt an obligation to agree. It was the only plan they had. As the taxi drew to a stop, Leo looked up at the bank's looming concrete building. It was as gloomy today as he remembered. Tau paid the driver with the money Leo had given him, and the pair stepped out into the road. Traffic swerved around them on the thin strip of tarmac.

"Give me two minutes," Tau said. "Two minutes, but no longer. Oh yeah, and wear this." Tau pulled a baseball cap from his pocket and tossed it to Leo. Tau strode out into the road. Horns and shouts of protest echoed from swerving vehicles.

Leo pulled the cap down low to shadow his face, then stepped backwards and ducked into the shadow of a doorway.

Tau climbed the stairs and walked into the bank. The room was as Leo had described. He looked around while he waited for his eyes to adjust to the gloom. Yellowed posters advertising the bank's services covered the dirty, white-washed walls, and a constant stream of dust skipped across the floor. In one corner stood an ATM, its lights blinking. The bank teller sat behind the desk talking aggressively on the phone.

Kathmandu Killers

Tau walked up to the desk, pulled out a grimy plastic chair and sat down. The teller finished her call and looked at him. Actually, Tau thought, it was more of a glare.

"I need to withdraw from a Worldwide Union account," Tau said in Nepalese. He fixed the most charming smile he could manage on his face.

The lady rose from her seat and collected a large pad from a filing cabinet behind her. It was the sort common in banks twenty years ago — pre-printed forms with carbon paper to copy in triplicate. Tau knew Kathmandu well enough not to be surprised that these things still existed.

"Number,"— she pointed to a box on the form — "photo ID and local address. It takes twenty-four hours." Her tone was slow and practiced. "How much?"

"Twenty-thousand dollars," Tau said, his smile unfaltering. "I bet that's the most you've had through here in a while."

"You would be surprised," the teller said flatly.

"Oh yeah?" Tau grinned, trying to warm her to his conversation. "What would someone be doing with more than that in this city?"

The lady shrugged and jabbed the pad with the pen.

"Fill in." She dropped the pen for Tau to use.

"I bet it was some old man who wanted to keep it under a mattress at home. I hope he doesn't get robbed."

Tau picked up the pen and started filling out the form. He paused before inventing a ten-digit number to make it appear like he'd thought about it.

The oscillating ceiling fan creaked on its circuit.

At that moment, as planned, Leo barged through the doors of the bank. He pretended not to see Tau and the bank teller as he looked around for the ATM. He needed to make it seem like he hadn't been there before. Tau snuck a look over his shoulder. With Leo's hair beneath the cap and his efforts to look baffled by the place, they just might get away with this.

"ID?" the lady asked, watching Tau complete the last box. She had so far ignored Leo, who now stalked toward the ATM.

Leo slipped one of The Best Kathmandu Guest House's business cards into the cash machine's slot. He jabbed at the keypad a few times.

"CARD ERROR" flashed on the screen.

"What the hell?" Leo said loudly, attracting the attention of both Tau and the bank teller. "What's it doing? You can't do this to me!"

Then, Leo started to hit the machine, whacking it

on its sides and top. He even kicked it twice, each time making sure the strike sounded worse than it actually was.

The bank teller shot up and shouted at Leo in Nepalese. She rushed over to interpose herself between Leo and the innocent machine.

Tau only had a few moments. He flicked back through the pad and looked for Allissa's name.

He scanned the first sheet. No luck.

The second. Still nothing.

The lady was trying to calm Leo, who continued to shout at the innocent ATM.

"It's got my card! Without that, I have nothing!" Leo slapped the top of the machine. Dust jumped from its metal surface.

On the third sheet, Tau saw what he was looking for.

Allissa Stockwell, written in large, curvaceous writing in blue ink.

36,588 USD.

Local address: Teku Guesthouse, Redcross Sedak, Kathmandu.

Tau closed the pad, got up, hurried down the steps and out into the street.

Leo allowed himself to be placated by the bank

teller. But, before she could recognize him, he turned and grumbled outside.

A minute later, down the road and out of sight of the bank, Tau and Leo caught up with each other.

"Did you get it?" Leo was the first to speak. He knew the answer.

"Did I get what?" Tau asked, his grin wide.

"An address? Did you get anything?" Leo's smile dropped, suddenly anxious.

"Of course!" Tau said after a dramatic silence. "Let's go."

20

Allissa turned, looked at the Teku Guesthouse, and smiled. How ever she felt personally, she was doing well. Her life, her existence, was benefiting the people around her. That brought her a contentment all the money, clothes and make-up of her youth had failed to.

In the warm afternoon sun, the guesthouse looked especially appealing. Allissa remembered the first time she'd walked across the small square and looked up at its brightly painted exterior.

Allissa turned and walked in the direction of the market. She was buying food for dinner while Fuli and Chimini looked after the guesthouse. They'd already checked in two more people that afternoon.

Inside the guesthouse, Chimini wandered out

from behind the reception desk and headed towards one of the bedrooms. "I'm going for a shower," she said in their native tongue. The temperature of the guesthouse reception was stifling. "Come and get me if you need anything."

Fuli nodded.

"Will you be okay?" Chimini asked.

Although Fuli managed okay when a young man checked in earlier, Chimini noticed the room key was passed across with shaking fingers.

Fuli nodded again.

Chimini wasn't gone long before footsteps echoed up the stairs. Fuli's smile vanished as two men walked into the reception area.

For a moment she was back there. The curtain, his voice, the smell of sour whisky on his breath. She slammed the memories away and tried to force a smile.

The first of the men was a westerner, skinny, tall and pale. The second, Indian, his skin tone darker than hers from long days spent in the searing sun.

Chimini had been teaching Fuli the English phrases she would need to work behind the reception desk, and she hurriedly racked her brain for them. She could do this.

The westerner was the first to speak. It was a

Kathmandu Killers

phrase she didn't understand. The Indian's translation a few seconds later surprised her.

"I'm looking for my sister."

The white man showed her a picture on his phone and Fuli recognized it immediately. She tried to hide her surprise. Men looking for you couldn't be a good thing.

"Not here," Fuli replied in Nepalese. "Never seen her."

The men regarded her with a steady look.

"Has she been here?" the white man asked, the Indian man translating.

"Not here," Fuli said again. She looked down at the large check-in book spread open on the desk.

"When did she leave?" he asked, persistent. Fuli felt them looking at her.

"Not here," she said for the third time.

"I'll give you one hundred dollars," the man said, showing her two fifty dollar bills, "if you can tell me where my sister is."

Fuli had never seen dollars before, although she knew they were worth a lot in the city. Some of the men had used them. She'd seen them changing hands, but they had been quickly pushed into a pocket or a bag as she'd entered.

"Any information you can give me would be very

helpful," the white man said, smiling and showing Fuli the photo again. "I really need to find her."

The white man picked up one of the guesthouse's business cards and scribbled a number down.

"Call me if you remember anything, and the one hundred dollars is yours."

He offered the card to Fuli, but she didn't take it. He put it down on the counter with the number facing her.

The pair turned and descended the stairs.

"Who was that?" Chimini asked as she opened the door from the bedroom. Her wet hair was wrapped in a towel.

"Someone looking for Allissa," Fuli said quietly, handing her the card. "Says he was her brother. I did not tell them anything."

"Well done," Chimini said, turning the card over in her hands. "People looking for you usually isn't a good thing."

"THERE'S something she's not telling us," Leo said as their coffee arrived. They sat in a small café across the square from the guesthouse.

"We don't have to rush," Tau said. "We can always come back here tomorrow."

They'd made progress, and that was good. Leo wasn't ready to give up for the day.

"I feel like she knew more than she was telling," Leo said, looking back across the square. Compared to the rest of Kathmandu, punctuated continuously with horns and traffic, this area was quiet. Leo liked it.

"It might just have been the translation," Tau said.

"No, there was more to it than that. I'm sure. It was her look of surprise when I showed her the picture. Something to do with her age, too. I think a girl of that age is more likely to lie for Allissa." Leo chased the thought out loud.

"You're just seeing what you want to," Tau said. "She was a bit confused, surprised by your questions. If she does know anything, maybe she'll call."

"I wouldn't count on it. If she knows Allissa, they're friends somehow, and I think women of that age stick together."

"Money can be tempting," Tau said.

"We offered one hundred dollars for information on someone who we know has thirty-five-thousand," Leo said, gazing out into the square. "I wouldn't count on it."

An hour later Leo and Tau walked into the restaurant with the Chinese lanterns. They took the same table which they'd been at the previous night and Tau ordered beers.

Leo had to be persuaded to even set foot inside the restaurant tonight. He couldn't have a repeat of the previous night's shenanigans. If he had a beer at all, it would strictly be just the one. The events of the day were already spinning around in his mind, and he needed some time to make sense of them.

Leo glanced around at the restaurant's other tables. Tourists from neighboring hotels lounged around them. Many wore colorful, baggy clothes which would seem inappropriate in their home countries. In Kathmandu, such attire bordered on an expectation. Not beyond hope that circumstance would bring him and Allissa to the same place, Leo checked each table in turn. Maybe a fortuitous stroke of luck was all he could hope for. As his eyes drifted from one diner to the next, he thought about Mya. Maybe one day a stoke of incredible luck would bring them to the same restaurant at the same time.

A man walked into the restaurant and settled at a table in the corner. There was something curious about him. Beneath a baggy, faded shirt, his chest seemed toned and there was something military about the way he scanned the scene. That was unusual, Leo thought, in someone traveling the world with little more than a backpack.

"Leo, Leo?" Tau said, holding out the bottle of beer.

"Yes? Sorry, thanks," Leo said, taking it and raising it in a toast.

Leo turned back to his thoughts as Tau ordered them another selection of the restaurant's creamy dishes.

Leo glanced again at the man in the corner. Something in Leo's consciousness rang with the image. It was as though their paths had crossed somewhere before. It was the sort of instinct Leo would normally put down as just a funny feeling. Right now, though, a funny feeling was all he had. That feeling could be the difference between success and failure.

Leo took a sip of the beer as he watched the man. Maybe he was here last night. They had been here twice, so for someone else to do the same was not unexpected. That was probably it.

"Right, I'm getting out of here," Leo said, finishing the beer a few minutes later.

"What, really?" Tau said. "I thought 'just one' was a figure of speech you Brits used just to come to the bar."

"It sometimes is," Leo said, grinning. "But today I

meant it." Leo slid a few notes beneath the bottle. "See you at nine in the reception. If we find Allissa tomorrow, I'll have two beers to celebrate."

"You go steady," Tau said, waving at Leo.

Leo crossed the restaurant, his mind on the events of the day and the sleep he desperately needed. The food and beer were weighing heavily. He just wanted to get back to his room and close his eyes.

The man in the corner raised his phone toward Leo and took a photo.

21

"He said he was my brother, and he was looking for me?" Allissa said to Fuli and Chimini as they prepared dinner. Chimini translated to Fuli, who thought for a couple of seconds before answering.

"Yes, he came in here, with a picture of you and asked if you had been here. He said he was your brother," Chimini added, toasting the spices in the pan. The small kitchen sang with their fragrance.

Allissa looked morosely towards the onions she was trying to cut as finely as Chimini required. She thought of her brother. The last thing she knew, he was working as a trader in London. When she left, he hadn't tried to contact her, not even once. Her sister Lucy had a couple of times. But, with a pang of guilt, Allissa had ignored the messages, ultimately changing mobile phones and closing down her social media profiles. She felt bad about that; none of this was Lucy's fault, nor Archie's. Yet, of the two of them, Archie hadn't seemed to care at all.

"What did he look like?" Allissa asked again. "Could you describe him in more detail?"

"White, westerner, thick dark hair, looked like a tourist," Chimini translated.

It didn't really sound like Archie. His hair was light, like Lucy's. Allissa couldn't rule it out for sure, though. Why would someone pretend to be him? It didn't make sense. Allissa looked down at the business card with the number scrawled on it, her curiosity growing.

If it was her brother, then she needed to know why he'd come. If it wasn't, she wanted to understand why someone would pretend to be him. She'd been away for two years, and no one had come after her. Why would they want to now?

Deep in thought, Allissa didn't notice the sharp, stinging pain in her left hand until blood spiralled across the chopping board. Allissa winced, dropped the knife and ran over to the sink. The stinging subsided as the juice from the onions washed away. Allissa inspected the tiny cut dramatically.

Kathmandu Killers

"Didn't they teach you how to chop onions in your expensive English schools?" Chimini said.

"Clearly not," Allissa said, a wry grin forming. "I'll write a strongly-worded letter about it."

Chimini instructed Fuli to wash and finish chopping the onion that Allissa had started, which she did with a speed Allissa couldn't fathom.

"I know what to do about these guys looking for me," Allissa said. "I think you should meet them again."

22

The night brought little rest for Leo. After two hours twisting and turning in the lumpy bed, he gave up trying to sleep and opened his eyes. So far, he couldn't normalize his body clock to the time difference. It didn't help that he couldn't stop turning events of the day through his mind.

First, Leo thought of the case. It felt positive that they had made progress and were closer than they had been that morning.

Allissa had been at the guesthouse, that much Leo knew. Now they needed to find out if the receptionist was lying, or if Allissa had moved on somewhere new.

Leo rubbed his stinging eyes. Allissa was close. He knew it. Something in the way the guesthouse receptionist acted told Leo she was near.

Lightning shimmered in the sky. It was still a long way off, but getting closer all the time.

Leo thought of Tau. He knew how Tau would feel tonight; lying alone in the bed he'd shared with Jem the night before. He'd likely not expected to meet anyone on holiday. Jem would have taken him by surprise, as would the feeling of loss when her taxi pulled away into the stream of traffic that afternoon.

Then, as usual, Leo thought of Mya. They'd not even gotten to say goodbye. She'd disappeared in the middle of a night that should have been perfect. A night that he'd waited for. A night that hadn't ended in the confirmation of their love, but in her disappearance. Leo felt sorry for Tau, but in a strange way, he also felt jealous. Tau's memories right now would never be this fresh or clear again. Those perfect moments would now fade, distorting in the unstoppable march of time.

THE NIGHT BROUGHT no rest for Kathmandu, either. The storm still tantalized, with far-off cracks of lightning rippling through layers of cloud.

Leo awoke after what felt like twenty minutes sleep. The sun filled his room with harsh light. He checked his phone. It was nearly eight am and his alarm was about to shriek. He lay still, listening to the hum of the air conditioner and passing footsteps in the corridor.

When his eyes brought the world into focus, he saw he'd received two messages during the night. One was from his mum. The formal tone of her messages always amused him.

Dear Leo, I trust you're having a successful time in Kathmandu...

She and his dad were seeing his sister and nephew for the weekend. He would no doubt have had an obligatory invitation if he'd been in Brighton.

The second message was from Stockwell.

Leo, I hope you'll have news soon.

Leo read it, then dropped the phone to the bed. He knew the job at hand and was working as quickly as possible. He didn't need the constant reminders.

Leo walked into the hotel reception ahead of the nine am arrangement and took a seat on one of the dusty sofas. The cheery receptionist insisted on holding conversation until Tau arrived.

If Tau had stayed out late last night, it didn't show. He waved at the receptionist with one hand while removing his sunglasses with the other.

"Alright boss," Tau said, crossing the room. "You feeling better after your early night? What's the plan for today?" Tau asked as they walked for the door.

"We'll go and ask around in some hotels, cafes and shops near the guesthouse," Leo said, shouting the second half of the sentence to compensate for the noise of the traffic. "We can't just sit about and wait."

"Coffee first though, mate," Tau said, pulling his sunglasses back over his eyes.

"Of course, if it helps with the hangover." Leo offered a smug grin.

A few minutes later, both cradling large coffees, Leo and Tau started the walk toward the Teku Guesthouse.

The morning passed quickly. The hotels, cafes, bars, guesthouses, hostels and shops were numerous, though none were informative.

"We only need one to have seen her," Leo said as they stepped back into the street from a tourist shop. Brass Buddhas shimmered in a diesel smelling haze.

Tau knew many places by location, if not by their name, owner and family history. Those he didn't, they stumbled upon. Just in one street they checked a hidden guest house occupying a floor in a residential building, a man selling bottled drinks from a cart and a large woman in a crimson sari selling leather wristbands and bangles.

"She was selling hash, too," Tau said as they walked away from the woman in the crimson sari.

"How did you know?" Leo turned to look at the woman, now talking with a pair of tourists.

"She's been around for years. She always stands right there."

"Don't the police do anything about it? Isn't it illegal?" Leo asked.

"Yeah sure, it's illegal. She's not doing any harm, though. Arrest her, and who's going to feed her family? Plus, she couldn't afford to get out. They might even be watching her now."

"What, watching and doing nothing?"

"Watching is not doing nothing." Tau laughed. "They'll be watching to see who she sells to. The buyers will have money, and the police like to see a few tourists in jail every now and then."

"So they'd arrest the tourists instead? That doesn't really seem fair."

"Look at it this way," Tau said, turning to face Leo on the busy road. "The police have to arrest someone, as it shows they're actively doing something about the drugs problem. They don't want to arrest her, though, because she has a family that needs looking after.

Kathmandu Killers

They can't catch the suppliers, because they're too clever and wealthy. The tourists just make easy pickings."

By the early afternoon, they'd had a conversation with every receptionist, shop owner, or street seller within a mile of the guesthouse. Leo had shown each of them the photo, and Tau had explained that they were looking for Leo's sister, and offering money if Tau thought it would help.

"You have to be careful who you offer money to," Tau explained. "People get easily offended about things like that."

But all this work, so far, had amounted to nothing. Some people said no swiftly, on more than one occasion shooing Leo and Tau away with the palm of a hand. Others thought for some time, flicking through hotel record sheets or inviting Leo and Tau to consult their security cameras. On those occasions, Tau intervened, suggesting that the hotelier or shop keeper check themselves and call if they found anything.

"Something will come up, don't worry," Tau said, in reassurance at Leo's obvious frustration.

"She could be pretty much anywhere," Leo grumbled. "Particularly if she doesn't want to be found. We'd have no chance."

"My mother used to say" – Tau became solemn —

"that the world is too crazy, too busy. People want everything now, now, now." He mimicked his mother's voice. "She said that when you really want something, you need to sit and think about the best way to get it. Running around never solved anything."

"Maybe," Leo said, trying not to sound skeptical. "I'm just not sure that works with missing people. They don't seem to return of their own accord."

"Well, it works when you lose something. I remember once, my dad lost something. We were turning the place upside down to find it. People were running everywhere. I remember my mum sat in a chair and watched for about an hour until we were all getting bored and frustrated. Then she got up, and went to a drawer that no one had checked. It was right there. I've no idea how she found it." Tau looked toward the window. "But since that day, I believe there's always some truth in sitting and thinking about a problem when you're out of ideas."

"Where do your parents live now?" Leo asked warmly.

Tau didn't have a chance to answer. Leo's phone rang, a long Nepalese number flashing on the screen.

Tau answered the call. The conversation moved quickly. Leo listened closely but couldn't decide if what Tau was saying sounded good or bad. After less than a minute, Tau hung up.

"That was the girl we saw at the Teku Guesthouse yesterday," Tau said. "Says she knows where Allissa is."

23

Allissa, Fuli and Chimini were in position ahead of the arranged four pm arrival of the two men. Allissa hid behind one of the bedroom doors and peered out at Chimini and Fuli at the reception desk. Chimini and Fuli spoke about the program on the small TV as though everything was normal. Allissa couldn't see the TV, but heard its indistinct chatter.

Four pm came and went in agonizing seconds.

Chimini had questioned whether it was a good idea to invite the men back into the guesthouse. Allissa thought it was unlikely the men would give up that easily, and Fuli didn't think they seemed dangerous. In fact, if anything, the description she'd given was complimentary. Even so, Chimini slid the sharpest kitchen knife they had beneath the checking-in book and Allissa leaned a large metal pole up against the wall beside her. Both women knew that it paid to be careful.

Allissa looked around the newly furnished room. Frustration welled up inside her. They'd achieved so much in the last few weeks, and cowering behind a bedroom door felt like a step in the wrong direction. She hadn't traveled halfway around the world to continue to run and hide.

She pulled the blinds aside and looked down out at the square. Shadows from the skeletal trees spread like fingers across the slabs as the sun began its descent.

That, she supposed, was the nature of running. You didn't get to decide when you stopped.

Footsteps echoed up the stairs behind her. Allissa crept back behind the door and peered out into the reception area. The girls were still behind the front desk. Everything looked normal. The footsteps drew closer. Allissa pushed the door gently closed to ensure she was out of sight.

Inane chatter reverberated from the TV.

"Hey, how are you?" Allissa heard someone say. It was a male voice. English. Neither Chimini nor Fuli replied.

Allissa smiled — the girls were going to make them work for it.

"You have some information for us? About Allissa?" the man said again, slow and simple.

Allissa pushed the door open an inch and peered out. She held her breath and willed her heart to beat more quietly. Fuli and Chimini watched the TV.

Two men approached the desk.

After a few seconds, as though waiting for a signal, Chimini pressed a button, silencing the TV. Stirring up a dislike for men, Allissa supposed, was easy for women like Fuli and Chimini.

"Why you want to see her?" Chimini asked.

"She is my sister."

"No, she is not," Chimini replied. "Her brother looks nothing like you."

The man shifted his weight from one foot to the other. Chimini's hand slid instinctively toward the concealed knife.

Allissa watched closely, Chimini had given away the fact she knew Allissa well enough to have talked to her since their last visit, but that didn't mean Allissa was still in Kathmandu. Allissa figured it was worth it to expose the man's lie.

Allissa's hand closed around the metal pole as she

Kathmandu Killers

watched the scene unfold. Although she hoped she wouldn't have to use it, the feel of the cold metal brought reassurance.

The white man cleared his throat. The larger, Nepali or Indian-looking man — Allissa couldn't tell from behind — stepped backward to give his friend some space.

"You're right. I lied," the man at the front said. His voice was soft and slow, like a promise. "I'm looking for her because her family are very worried about her. They haven't heard from her for a long time. They just want to know if she's alright." He paused for a moment. Fuli looked toward Chimini.

"They haven't asked me to bring her home or anything," he reassured the women. "I'm just here to check that she's alright. Then I can let them know she's fine, and be out of your way."

Chimini didn't reply. In the momentary pause, Allissa thought Fuli had described the man well. From the back, he was slight and pale, with big messy hair. He was clearly an inexperienced tourist.

"Why should we help you find her?" Chimini asked after the silence had passed its breaking point.

"You don't have to help me," he said. "You don't have to, but..." He paused, making a choice. "I'm someone who knows what it's like to lose someone. I know what the sleepless nights and unanswered questions do to a person." He paused again, inhaling, exhaling. "My girlfriend went missing two years ago, and I think about her every day. Every day I want to know where she is. So, I help other people whose loved ones are missing, too."

Allissa watched through the gap in the door. Someone looking for her wasn't a good thing, yet this man wasn't the thick-necked thug she would have expected her dad to employ. Allissa had seen those types around the house when she was younger. Maybe there was more to this than she'd initially expected. She definitely wasn't expecting the soft words of the man who looked like he hadn't yet grown into his skin.

"When Allissa's father asked me to find his missing daughter," he continued, putting the palms of his hands on the top of the reception desk, "I felt like I had to help."

When Allissa's dad asked me to find his missing daughter...

The sentence bubbled in Allissa's ears.

His missing daughter.

It rose like anger. A flame in a cave, invading the darkness.

His missing daughter.

How could she be his, after what he had done? He surrendered his claim to her when...

The words came out before Allissa realized she was speaking.

"My dad's screwing with you as well then..."

24

———————

Leo wasn't used to success. He was used to disappointment, apologies and on occasion an *almost there*. Success was something he had very little experience of.

Over the last few days he had become so focused on how he was going to find Allissa, that he didn't actually know what he was going to do if, and when, he did. Talk to her, he supposed, then tell her dad she was all good, collect his money, and get home.

The moment before hearing the voice, Leo's attention was fixed on the young ladies behind the reception desk. Their hazel eyes showed nothing but innocence, a profound childlike purity which Leo felt drew the honesty from him.

"My dad's screwing with you as well then."

Kathmandu Killers 149

The bottom fell from Leo's stomach, and a lump appeared in his throat when he heard the voice. Whilst he didn't recognize the voice, he knew instantly whose it was.

Leo turned and stood face-to-face with the woman he'd been sent to find. Allissa Stockwell. Alive and well. Right here, in the flesh.

She was taller than Leo had imagined, yet it was unmistakably her. She had dark skin, darker than in the photos he'd seen, the result of months in a warm climate. Her hair was dark, contrasting a pair of bright, expressive eyes which now burned in anger.

"My dad's screwing you over too, is he?" Allissa repeated.

When Leo came to his senses, his jaw opened slightly. "I hope not," he replied, shaking himself back into focus. "He's already paid me to find you. So, I suppose if anyone was screwing anyone, I was screwing him until just now."

"He'll have something prepared. You wait. When he's finished, you see how long it takes to drop you," Allissa said, her voice serrated.

"As I just said to your friends here," Leo said, indicating the receptionists, "I'm not here to force you to go home or to do anything. I just want to talk to you so I can let your father know you're alive and well."

"You can do that now. Here I am."

"I have a few things I'd like to ask you. If that's okay? Is there somewhere we could talk?"

"All the rooms here are full."

"We can go to the café across the road? Coffee? Something stronger?"

Allissa glanced at the two women standing behind Leo.

"Yeah, alright," she said. "But not for long. We have customers."

"Let me start by telling you a little about me," Leo said as they sat opposite each other in the café. Tau had gone back to the hotel, his work complete.

"I heard you telling Chimini about your missing girlfriend. Is that true? Or was that a lie to get her to talk? Like saying you were my brother?"

"Totally true," Leo said.

"Did you try to find her?"

"Yes. I've tried everything. At the time she disappeared I tried to get help from the local police, but they were useless. They tried to pin her disappearance on a guy who worked at the hotel. I couldn't get any proper answers. There are only a few ways off the island, so someone must have known something." Leo pulled himself back into the present. "I've spent the last two years looking for her online. I set up a website, Missing People International. That's how your dad found me..."

"You help a lot of people like this?"

"I help a lot of people through the website. I tell them where to go and who to contact, but I've never helped anyone like this before... or actually found them."

"So, why now?"

"I lost my job a few weeks ago. Your dad approaching me was actually quite good timing, I suppose."

"What did you do?"

"I was a journalist at a local newspaper."

"How did you lose it?"

"The editor thought I recorded a court case, got the paper into loads of trouble. It wasn't me, I know that's completely illegal and would never have done that. It was another guy who worked there."

"Convenient, that is, isn't it?" Allissa said, folding her arms. She softened with the higher ground.

"What?"

"You can do something my dad wants, you lose your job, then he approaches you to help him."

Leo hadn't thought of it that way before.

"Why did you get blamed for filming the court case?" Allissa asked.

"The paper's owner thought I was the only person with the social media passwords. Turns out another guy, Callum, had got them somehow and logged in on his phone."

Allissa looked beyond Leo and out into the square. Leo leaned forward.

"Callum," Allissa said thoughtfully. "My brother had a friend called Callum and last I heard he was a journalist. Dad was using him for leaking all sorts of government info, mostly lies about his rivals. Callum was doing well out of it, though, because it sold papers. What was his second name?"

Leo had to think. The world of Brighton, the incessant rain, the newspaper... It all seemed a lifetime ago.

"Martins?"

"That was it, I'm sure!"

Leo looked at Allissa. For the second time a lump formed in his throat. His breathing quickened. He inhaled deeply to calm himself.

"If he's got all these connections I don't understand why he would send someone who'd never done this before?" Leo asked. "Surely it would be better to send someone experienced. He could certainly afford to pay for it."

"Because he's afraid they'd do him over, maybe? They could learn why he wanted to find me so much, then blackmail him or something."

"Well, why wouldn't I do that?"

"Because you're an out-of-work journalist who's still bitter about the loss of an ex-girlfriend. No one would believe what you're saying."

"What could he be so scared about me knowing?"

Allissa looked at him, straight and hard. Her voice, angry and bitter. "What he did to my mum."

Lights in the windows surrounding the small square flickered on as afternoon dissolved to evening. Allissa gazed up at the guesthouse on the top floor of the building opposite, its bright colors smothered by the coming night.

Allissa knew that she didn't have to tell Leo anything. There was no obligation. Yet he was a victim too, in a way.

"I found out two years ago, and haven't been back since," Allissa said. "I can't bear to see him. And he knows I'll tell anyone I want because she was my mum."

Leo said nothing.

"As you probably know, I grew up with my father,

step-mum and half-brother and sister. To be honest, they're lovely. Lucy, Archie and me used to get on so well. It was clear I was different from them, we all knew it, but it wasn't a problem. No one was bothered. In many ways, I was very lucky. I went to great schools and had good friends. I'd never wanted for anything." Allissa paused, finished her drink, then signaled for another. This time she asked for a beer.

"I knew Eveline wasn't my mother. They'd told me that from a very young age. I assumed, when I was old enough to understand, that dad had an affair with my mother. Then after my mum died, I came to live with them. That wasn't the whole story. I used to ask dad about my mum, and he used to tell me things. I realized that Eveline didn't like it, so I stopped. When dad and I were alone together, though, I'd ask. He'd only tell me little things, but to me, they were so important. All I really know about her is from those moments. She was from Kenya — they met while dad was over there. He went a few times with work and they struck up a relationship. He can be pretty charming by all accounts. He gave me a photo of her. She was beautiful. Tall and elegant, with an incredible smile. In one picture she's standing with other people; they must be my relatives, I just don't know who. He told me — and it's what I believed for so long — that she'd gone back to Kenya to see some family, and that while she was there she had an accident and died. That was a lie."

Beers arrived at the table, and Allissa took a long gulp. Tears sparkled in her eyes.

Leo leaned forward, hanging on each word.

"Then, one evening, things weren't going well at uni. I got in an argument with someone. I can't remember who now, but I went home. I just needed to get some space. I let myself into the house as I normally would. No one was home. Lucy and Archie were away too. After a while, dad and Eveline came in and I went to surprise them. It sounds stupid now. I heard them talking from outside the kitchen door. Something in their voices made me stop and listen…"

"You're doing it again, aren't you?" Eveline said, her voice raspy, angry, and violent.

Stockwell didn't reply.

"You just couldn't help yourself, could you? I knew you were doing it, but why?"

Silence.

"Didn't you have enough of that last time? You knew the trouble that got us in to. How many favors did you need to pull to make that mistake disappear."

Hidden behind the kitchen door, a jolt moved through Allissa's body. The tectonic plates of understanding shifted in her mind. The blood drained from her face.

"Well, I did sort it, didn't I?" Stockwell said, his voice a violent whisper.

"You sorted it? You sorted it? You pushed the poor woman off the terrace. We had a dead body in our garden. What if one of the children had come back? What if you hadn't been able to cover it up... what if your man at border control hadn't been able to..." Eveline let out an anguished sob.

"Oh Eveline, listen to yourself. Have you got no faith in me. This is what I do, I sort things out. I already had the record of her leaving the country arranged. It was all so simple, arranged ahead of time. There really was no risk."

"No risk! No risk!" Eveline screamed, her voice hoarse. "Is that the only way you can think about this, risk to yourself. What about Allissa?"

Behind the door, Allissa shuddered. She wrapped her arms around her body as though the motion would stop her physically falling into pieces.

"Allissa has everything she needs. That was always my intention. If that woman had stopped interfering when our family, then..."

"That woman had no choice. Allissa was her daughter, her only daughter."

Allissa drew a deep breath. She'd heard enough. Something told her to get out now, before they realized she was here. A shudder of fear shook her to the core.

Silently she padded out from behind the door and crossed the hall. She slung on her coat and slipped out through the front door.

Driving away she looked back at Stockwell Manor in the rearview mirror. It would be several years until she returned.

LEO WATCHED Allissa wipe a napkin across her face. He felt as though he'd not taken a breath in minutes.

"The man's a monster," Allissa said. Jewels sparkled in her eyelashes. "After hearing that, I knew I had to learn the truth about what happened to my mother. It took a while, but eventually I found my auntie living in London. I'd stayed with her and my mum when I was little, until he took me. There were photos of me as a baby on their walls."

Allissa stifled a sob with a swig of beer.

"My auntie told me that for five years my mum

tried to get me back. She spent every penny she had battling his lawyers, but nothing helped. Every application was rejected, and every time she tried to get near, his security team were on hand. She knew I was there, and she couldn't get to me. After all of that, when my mum was almost out of hope, she got a message from Stockwell saying that he finally wanted to talk. Of course, she went straight there. The next thing my auntie learns, mum's been killed in a protest back in Kenya. Somehow he had got a contact in border control to make it look like she'd left the country. He even put her car in the long stay car park at Heathrow. My auntie never believed it, and nor did I."

Allissa's body shook with grief. She wrapped her arms across her chest and closed her eyes. Leo moved around the table and pulled her head towards him. He didn't know the girl, she didn't know him. But he was there. He was involved.

"Let's get out of here," Allissa said after the tears subsided. "I need a change of scene."

25

Leo and Allissa walked into the sepia glow of the restaurant with the Chinese lanterns. At the tables, drinkers and diners chatted noisily as relentless waiters replenished their food and drinks.

Leo led Allissa to the back of the restaurant where he and Tau had sat the previous night. Allissa ordered two beers from a passing waiter.

"How come you ended up here then?" Leo asked.

"I was traveling through, like most people," Allissa said. "I worked my way through India, making it up as I went along. The only thing I knew was that I didn't want to go home. I didn't really like Kathmandu at first. One afternoon I got talking to a group of people who were here working for a charity. That's when things changed." Allissa told Leo of her trip out to the remote villages of Nepal which spawned the idea of the guesthouse.

The beers arrived, and they both paused to drink.

"I like how you've used money from your dad to do something so good," Leo said. "There's an irony there."

"Yeah, he may be a monster, but he's a very rich monster. He'd given me a trust fund which I knew was worth a lot of money. I used it to set up the guesthouse. The girls were victims, and now they're business people. It's taken a while, but the place has finally come together. The girls know what they're doing, and the first few guests have arrived. I'm not sure they even need me there."

Allissa let the words settle.

"It's such a good thing," Leo said, catching Allissa's eye.

"Yeah, it's gone really well."

"Don't the police or authorities do anything for these girls?"

"Yes, well, they are getting better. They used to just ignore the problem. There's a massive stigma attached to prostitution in Nepalese society. In the past the authorities would brush it under the carpet by pretending it wasn't happening. That would leave the victims with nowhere to go. Fortunately in the last few months they've really started to crack down. A couple of men from the gangs are now on long prison sentences. Hopefully that's made an example to those still doing it."

Leo nodded.

"It's started to make a difference to the girls, too. That's the important thing. Just the idea that the authorities care about them has reduced their shame."

Leo looked across the restaurant beyond Allissa. The lanterns swung, pulled by the turbulent air against their fixings. Whilst the thunder had stopped for now, the pressure in the air prophesized its return. Maybe later the rain would finally make it to the city.

Tau sauntered into the restaurant. His face lit up when he saw Leo and Allissa.

Leo beckoned him over.

"I wouldn't have found you without this guy," Leo said, pointing at Tau.

"It was nothing really," Tau said, shrugging. He introduced himself formally to Allissa.

Ever the gentleman, Leo thought.

"Leo told us he was looking for you a couple of nights ago," Tau said. "He made it sounds like such a task, I figured I'd have to help him out."

"I don't know what all the fuss was about," Leo said, smiling at the gentle teasing.

"It was good working with you," Tau said. "I knew you'd do it."

"Hey," Allissa interjected. "I know this might have been just a case to you private eyes, but I am right here, you know."

"Sorry." Tau turned to Allissa. "It must make you feel important, though, no? Having people out there looking for ya?"

"No really. It's pretty scary, actually. One of the things I liked about this city was that it felt so far from home. So far, that no one would make journey. I knew that withdrawing that money would be problematic, but I figured it was worth the risk." Allissa stared forlornly at the beer. She wiped some of the moisture away from the bottle. "Now it feels as though anyone could turn up at any time, you know? Like I'm not safe anymore. Maybe it's time to move..."

"Alright guys, mind if I join ya?"

Allissa was cut off mid-sentence by a new voice nearing their table.

Six weeks until Mya's disappearance. Agra, India.

Kathmandu Killers

· · ·

Leo had wanted to visit the Taj Mahal ever since he had seen a photo of it as a child. To him, each grainy black and white pixel of that photograph hinted at exciting and undiscovered lands.

Now, as he and Mya got ready for an evening of food and drinks, with their plan to get up early to see the Taj at sunrise, his excitement built to fever pitch. In his mind's eye he imagined that he and Mya were there already, looking up at the world's greatest memorial to love and loss. It was a day he knew would be unforgettable, especially with what he had planned. What could be better than asking the most important question of his life outside the monument which signified love like no other in the world?

He envisioned it then, bent to one knee, the eminent marble domes of the Taj in the background as he presented Mya with the ring. The ring he had been hiding for the entire trip.

"Would you..." the words stuttered in the turbulent anxiety of his mind. "Would you..."

As Mya took a shower, Leo rummaged through his bag for the ring. He'd kept it carefully buried amongst his stuff for almost a month, but tonight he would need to hide it close. He would need it tomorrow.

Leo felt the box at the bottom of his bag and pulled it out. He intended to leave the box behind and just take the ring on its own.

Snapping the box open, he peered inside. The three diamonds glinted angrily, as though Leo had disturbed their slumber.

What if they had metal detectors and bag searches on the way in? He thought, fear stabbing at his chest. He didn't want Mya to see the ring before the moment was right.

"Shower's free," Mya said, walking into the bedroom wrapped in a towel. "It's warm, get in now."

"Thanks," Leo replied, closing the box and stuffing it deep inside the backpack.

Tomorrow, he thought. Tomorrow would be perfect.

A few minutes later they left the hotel and walked side-by-side through Agra's hurried streets. The smells, colors and vibrancy of India surrounded them. It was a city like many others — throbbing traffic, spices, gabbling conversation.

Up ahead, a long-horned cow sauntered the street. A group of tourists paused and reached for their cameras.

"Look at that," Mya said, pointing out a sign on a building to the left.

Rooftop bar and restaurant, views of Taj Mahal.

"Shall we?" she said, crossing the road before waiting for a reply.

They climbed a dusty stairwell, passing a different guesthouse or residence on each floor. On the final flight, a strip of sky appeared above them.

Standing on the skyline, amid the jumble and tussle of Agra, the Taj revealed herself. Domes and minarets in ivory white took on the changing hue of the glowing air, shining as they had every day for five-hundred years.

Mya stepped forwards, entranced by the Taj on the skyline..

Despite his lifelong desire to see the Taj, that was just a building. Buildings don't give people hope, or optimism, or love; they can inspire it, but those feelings only come from other people. Leo gazed longingly at Mya.

In that moment, Leo wondered why people felt the compulsion to travel at all. It wasn't because of the sights and sounds and smells of the place. You could see or smell things anywhere, right? Was it be because of the people? He thought not, because the world was full of people. You can meet new and interesting people every day.

Watching Mya blink away the dry evening, Leo

knew it was because of the feeling. That feeling. When you came to a new place like this, you left your feelings behind and opened your heart and mind to the raw struggles of others. Sometimes that was understanding the people you met, and sometimes it was those you traveled beside.

26

"I see you've got a spare seat." Leo, Tau and Allissa looked toward the sound. "This place is pretty busy... mind if I join ya?"

"Yeah, no problem, mate," said Tau, indicating the empty seat next to Allissa. Beers had arrived, and the three were going through them quickly.

"I'm Miles." The stranger offered a thick, tanned hand around the table. He spoke in a broad Australian accent.

"What brings you here?" Tau asked after the introductions had been made.

"Living the dream, mate." Miles laughed and ordered a beer from a passing waiter.

"What do you think of the place?" Tau asked.

"It's not as good as last time."

"When was that?"

"1978," Miles said. "I was twenty. Younger than you guys I'd say. Living in South London at the time. Me and my brother bought a van. It already had about a hundred-thousand miles on it. Yellow, and rusty as hell. My brother knew a bit about engines, so he fixed it up nice. I painted it. We got mattresses in the back, sleeping bags, and one morning we set off. We were on the ferry to Calais at eight forty-five."

Leo, Allissa, and Tau listened.

Miles pushed a curl of grey hair behind his ear. "We didn't even know where we were going, but we set off. You can't do that anymore. Everyone knows where they're going now. Got these *sat navs* and that. We just knew we had to go east. Got a compass glued to the dash. So, we kept going east." Leo thought there might have been some opposition to Miles dominating the conversation, but there wasn't. Miles' beer arrived, and he drank a third straight off the bat.

"The roads were full of hippies back in those days. We drove down through Turkey into Iran. Didn't stay in Tehran long, just passed through. They didn't have alcohol. Then into Afghanistan, Pakistan, India. Then we chose to head north and came here. It's such an incredible feeling to come that far overland. You really get a true impression of how small the world is and how many different people live across it. We left a raining, grey London one day, and four months later rolled into Kathmandu in the same battered old van. I remember it like it was yesterday."

"How long did you stay?" Tau asked.

"Stayed here for a month. It was the sort of place you just couldn't leave. Then we went back to India. We'd planned to drive home, but by that point it wasn't looking too good in Iran or Afghanistan, so we bummed about for a few weeks. One morning we got a letter from our parents with two airline tickets. They'd never been that keen on us going. They'd seen Iran on the news and assumed the whole of Asia was like that. Using the tickets felt a bit like selling out, having come all that way in the van. In the end, we turned up at Bombay airport on a Monday morning and landed back in London that evening. And the worst thing,"— Miles took a sip of the beer — "the worst thing is, I don't even have any pictures of it. I didn't have a camera back then. All I've got to remember it by is what's in here." He tapped the side of his head.

Miles fished a pack of cigarettes from his breast pocket. He offered them around the table. Tau took one, the others said no. Miles shook out a cigarette for himself and then produced a silver cigarette lighter from another pocket.

"That's a fancy looking lighter," Allissa said, admiring the glinting silver box.

"S.T. Dupont. Worth an arm and a leg, I tell you. Fiftieth birthday present to myself," Miles said, lighting a cigarette.

He passed the lighter to Allissa who turned it over in her hands then passed it to Tau who lit his cigarette.

"How did you find fitting back into normal life after your travels?" Leo asked.

Miles laughed, exhaling a plume of smoke. "Yeah, that was hard. Had to get a job. My first real job. A year later, I was married and had a baby on the way. The eighties came, and the world felt different. It wasn't quite as fun anymore. We were lucky to do it when we did." Miles looked into the middle-distance, then continued to tell of his three children, how they'd moved to Australia when his oldest was eight, and how he now had a collection of grand-children.

"Your wife didn't fancy coming with you?" Tau asked.

"She died last year," Miles said, regaining focus on the table. "It was a total shock. One day she was complaining of a headache, which was totally unlike her. She took a few painkillers and went to bed. She just didn't wake up again. She'd had a stroke during the night. After a while, we knew she wasn't coming back."

The lanterns around the bar trembled. The night had taken on a chill. Leo drained his beer and added it to the pile of empties.

Leo watched Miles carefully for a moment. Maybe it was just the conversations of conspiracy he and Allissa had shared earlier in the evening, but something about this situation made him feel uneasy.

"You know, I always said I'd come back here," Miles continued, looking around. "My wife said she'd come with me. That's one of the reasons I had to come back. She'd heard so many stories and wanted to see the places for herself. We kept saying we would."

"Well, you're here now mate," said Tau. "It's good to have met you."

Leo looked at Allissa. She seemed content. Maybe the company was the distraction she needed.

"You know all the cool places to go around here, then?" Tau asked.

"I'm sure it was different in those days," Allissa said.

"Oh yeah," said Miles, his expression brightening. "When we were here before there was the most incredible restaurant. We went as often as we could. I've eaten at restaurants all around the world, and I don't think I've ever had a meal as good as at that place."

"What was it called?" asked Allissa.

"You know what, I've no idea. I'm not even sure it had a name. But I don't think it was far from here."

Miles looked left and right as though looking for the place right there. A waiter arrived with fresh beers and collected the stack of empties.

"You reckon you could find it?" Tau asked.

Miles thought for a while and asked a couple of questions about landmarks and street names.

"Yeah, sure," he said after a moment, smiling. "Of course I could."

"Well then... we're going," Tau said.

Out in the street, it was clear the group had already sunk a few beers. Their voices got louder as they walked. As the evening pushed on the traffic had dwindled to a trickle of cars, bikes and taxis. Of course, the hungry cows still roamed freely.

Tau and Miles walked in front, laughing at each other's tales of traveling in obscurity and swigging beers they'd bought 'for the road'. Although Miles was taller than Tau, he walked with a slight stoop. With Tau's upright and boyish posture, they were almost the same height walking side-by-side.

Leo and Allissa followed the rocking pair.

"You don't mind coming, do you?" Leo asked.

"Seriously, if I didn't want to be here, I'd already be gone. I'll come for a bit of food then head back. The girls will be alright on their own for the evening. Plus, these guys are entertaining." Allissa pointed to Tau and Miles waiting beneath a rare working streetlight.

Miles dug out a pouch of tobacco and began to roll a cigarette. With the flare of a master magician he produced a bud of cannabis, broke it across the tobacco and then rolled it tight. He put it to his lips, fished out the Dupont lighter, and lit up.

"You know what I'd like to see," Miles said, his expression turning somber. "I would love for everyone in the western world to be able to experience more of places like this." He waved the spliff around, then passed it to Tau. "That would make the world a much nicer place, don't you think?" He asked no one in particular.

For what it was worth, Allissa agreed. She'd been surrounded by excess, intolerance and greed for most of her life, but had only realized it after visited places like this. She knew that it wasn't that she grew up around bad people, just the system they were born into taught them that material possessions were a normal measure of success.

Standing beneath the streetlight, surrounded by

people she'd only just met, Allissa remembered something Chimini had said to her in the first village they'd visited. In that village, Allissa had felt shocked by the abject poverty, and surprised by the apparent contentment of the villagers. *We're all suffering somehow. The only difference is choosing what to do about it.'*

"That's the shame, isn't it?" Tau said. "The people who could really benefit from this would never do it."

Miles nodded and wandered off, further into the gloom.

"I know it's around here somewhere, I remember this street. I'm sure of it," Miles said, his voice booming from the darkness. "It was a long time ago, but I knew I'd be coming back."

Miles walked on and turned into a passage that was even darker and thinner than before. The passage was so narrow that a car would struggle to fit down it, especially with the dark mounds of piled boxes and rubbish either side. The group picked their way forward using only the light seeping from windows high above.

"Do you know where you're going?" Tau shouted towards Miles.

"Nope!" came the reply from somewhere up ahead.

Tau laughed.

Kathmandu Killers

"We gotta look for a light," Miles said. "It used to be exactly the same as this, I think. There always used to be a light hanging above the door. That's how we knew where it was."

"We look a bit lost to me," Leo said from another part of the darkness.

"Do you know the greatest thing I've ever heard?" Miles said, his words starting to slur. "It was the Dalai Lama talking to some journalist in a suit. The journalist asked him about the meaning of life. He thought for a few seconds, then said that he didn't know."

Tau laughed.

"If the wisest dude in the world says it's okay not to know the answer sometimes, then that's alright for me."

"You've got to look for the light," Miles said again, stumbling blindly.

Leo was beginning to think this was a bad idea. Each turn had taken them down a narrower passage. Now they were walking single file through the darkness, following a man who'd not been here for forty years.

"There it is! I've found it!" Miles' voice came from somewhere up ahead. "I told you I still knew the way. All those years I've been planning to come back here!"

Leo could just about make out Miles standing at a

crossroads and pointing to the left. Leo and Allissa caught up with him and gazed into the inky shadows. Concrete structures towered on all sides.

Then, Leo saw the light. Above a doorway, a bare bulb hung like the final fruit on a dying vine. Miles strode toward it without a word.

Leo glanced at Allissa and Tau.

As Miles neared the door, it swung open. Without a backward look, Miles ducked and disappeared inside. Leo, Tau and Allissa exchanged glances.

Tau rushed forward and vanished beneath the bulb too.

"What do you think?" Leo asked Allissa.

"We've come this far." Allissa looked around, then started toward the door. "We might as well go and see what all the fuss is about."

Leo hurried after her. Together they paused and looked up at the hanging bulb.

Leo swallowed, his throat dry. He turned and looked back at the alleyway behind him.

Before he had a chance to say another word, Allissa ducked into the gloom of the restaurant.

"I hope this doesn't turn out to be a bad idea," Leo muttered, following the others inside.

"I told you I'd find it," Miles said. A waiter showed

them towards a table at the back of the small dining room.

"We never doubted ya," said Tau. "Looking forward to this."

A waiter delivered cutlery and a stack of napkins.

"I was here in 1978!" Miles said.

The waiter nodded nonchalantly.

Leo slumped into the chair and looked around. The restaurant had less than ten tables, each one lit by a single hanging bulb. The tables were close enough together that the waiters had to be careful when walking between them. Surprisingly, considering how difficult it had been to find the place, most of the tables were full.

Leo was reminded of something Mya used to say, '*the more difficult it is to get somewhere, the better it is when you do.*'

"We need to have the Himalayan Lamb," Miles said. "It's amazing. It comes from the mountains where the air is fresh, and the grass is clean. It's really difficult to get, but somehow this restaurant does it. That's what we always used to have."

The waiter arrived with bottles of beer and Miles made the order.

"How you feeling about Jem today?" Leo asked, shuffling to find comfort in the low seat.

"Yeah, alright. Sad to see her go, but I'll see her in a few weeks."

"What's that?" Miles asked.

"Tau's had a bit of a romance, haven't you mate?"

"Well, we just spent a bit of time together," Tau said, reddening.

"Tell us about her…" Allissa said.

Leo grinned at Tau's discomfort.

"Yeah, she's a nice girl. Very nice, actually."

"Details," Allissa prompted.

"We met in Varanasi and traveled together for a couple of weeks. You know when something just feels easy, like it's meant to be? It's been great. Totally didn't expect that to happen."

"Apparently they've not been without each other," Leo said.

"Nice one, mate," Miles said. "You gonna see her again?"

"We're going to try. We'll see."

"How do you feel about that?" Leo asked.

"I'm just happy it happened." His voice took on a softer tone. "Right now, I'd love to see her again, but time will tell."

The lamb arrived ten minutes later. It thudded to the table in a thick metal dish. To Leo, hungry from the day's exertions, it looked incredible. The dish was full of meat, some on the bone, some not. It hissed and spat as it cooled. The four diners shared glances of excitement.

Miles was the first in, abandoning cutlery and diving in with fingers and thumbs. Tau was next, going for a large bone that rose from the top of the dish. He picked it up and gnawed the supple lamb, pausing every few bites for a swig of beer. Leo and Allissa followed with fingers, thumbs and teeth.

Two groups got up from their tables on the other side of the room and lumbered under the weight of heavy meals towards the door. A handful of customers remained, some eating, others now slouched in their chairs.

"Man, this is taking me back!" Miles said, pausing mid-bite, a piece of lamb held by its unusually long bone in his clenched paw. "This is exactly how it was all those years ago. It's mad to think the last time I tasted this lamb I was twenty! All the things that have happened since. It's amazing the way life works sometimes."

Leo removed the last piece of lamb with his fork and examined the dish it was served on. The dish was long and thin, curved at the edges and rounded to a point at each end. Leo lifted it briefly from the table. It was heavy too.

"That was really good," Tau said, chewing the last chunk of meat and then leaning back to rest his stomach. Miles adopted the same slumped position. Allissa skewered the remaining onions with her fork.

"Yeah, decent," Miles said. A satisfied lull settled over the table.

On the other side of the restaurant, two men climbed to their feet. One stretched and scratched his hanging stomach while the other dropped a few notes on the table. They walked to the door and out into the night.

"I told ya it was amazing," Miles said, throwing his left arm backwards. "You guys had almost lost faith, yet here we are."

The waiter came to clear the table. He carried the dishes two at a time.

Tau ordered more beers.

As one of the waiters lumbered off through the darkness carrying the dishes, another approached. His smile was a radiating half-disc in the glow from the hanging bulbs.

"Excuse me," he said. "As you are special customers, we would like to offer you smoke as our gift. Would you like?"

27

"Yes, we do," Miles declared. "You guys haven't experienced the best part of this place yet."

The restaurant was almost empty now. The only other customers were a pair of tourists sorting unfamiliar bundles of money at the table by the door.

"I remember last time," Miles continued. "We spent the whole afternoon eating, drinking, and smoking in this place. We came in about midday, and it was after midnight before we left."

The others said nothing. Leo took a sip of the beer. It was cool and tasted especially good with the latent, lingering spice of the lamb.

"You know something I've realized," Miles' said.

"What?" Leo said.

"Loads of things in life are rubbish."

"What do you mean?" Tau asked, laughing.

"I mean that loads of the things we work for are pointless. This is total freedom we're feeling now. It's what I had back in my twenties before mortgages, hire purchase and package holidays. Yes, you might have a great house and a fast car, but is it worth giving your life up for? All you really need is a place to sleep, something to eat and clothes to wear, that's it. Why do you need that new car or the big TV when you're missing the opportunities to come to cool places and do cool things?"

Tau nodded in agreement.

Miles grinned, almost malevolently.

The waiter arrived with a large shisha pipe and stood it on the floor next to the table. The pipe was almost as tall as the sitting diners. The waiter lit the coals and then drew on one of the hoses. The coals glowed like the red eyes of a devil. The waiter pulled on the pipe again and the water inside the pipe bubbled. The smoke smelled pungent and sweet. It was like nothing Leo had experienced before.

The waiter sucked on the hose again. The smoke came through now, drifting through the air in a cloud. The waiter gave each of the diners a hose, stood back up, and returned to the kitchen.

"Nah, I totally get that," Miles said, he glanced at

his watch in the darkness. "But unfortunately I gotta head off. Can't do the late nights like you young things." The Australian climbed to his feet.

"Maybe see ya around," Tau said.

"Bit strange," Leo said, watching Miles walk through the restaurant and out through the door.

"What's that?" Allissa asked.

"He was so excited about this so-called special smoke, then when it arrived, he left." That distant flicker of worry moved in Leo's gut again.,

"It's right what he was saying though, isn't it," Tau said, his words slurring. "You know, those people who are obsessed with taking pictures of themselves in front of everything? Some people we traveled with seemed to just be there for the monument selfie. They weren't bothered about getting to know the people or the culture. They were trying to own the world, not just be part of it. That's just not what it's all about."

Leo shook his head, trying to let himself relax.

"People just trying to own the world, I reckon," Tau continued, stumbling over the words. "You can't own it, just be shaped by it. Guys, this is top," Tau said, indicating the pipe.

Leo and Allissa hadn't touched the hoses on their side of the table.

"You need to try it," Tau insisted.

"I'm not sure," Leo said. "It just doesn't…"

"Yeah, come on, man," Tau said. "You're in Nepal. This is what the place is all about."

Leo looked at the hose. He felt hazy enough from the beer and the smoke in the air. Smoking whatever this was felt uncomfortable, foreign and dangerous. Allissa didn't seem keen either.

"Let me tell you about this guy Jem and I met in India," Tau said. "He was telling us about where he'd been before… Laos, or somewhere like that. Anyway, he'd traveled for days to see this big old waterfall. It did look pretty special to be fair. He showed us the pictures. I asked him what the water was like. He said he didn't like swimming. What an idiot! You can't travel for days to see a waterfall and not go in the water, that's just not how it happens! Sometimes, whether you like swimming or not, you've got to jump in the water, because you might not ever go back there again."

Tau was right, Leo knew it, and he knew that's exactly what Mya would say too.

With her voice echoing in his mind, Leo picked up the hose and drew cautiously on the sweet-smelling smoke. Allissa did the same.

"Yeah man, jump in," Tau said. "The water's good!"

Leo sucked smoke through the hose. The angry

red eyes of coal sparked, and the smoke filled his lungs. He would just have a little. A taste.

A warm rush covered him, like a wave from a tropical ocean.

Breathe in, hold, and out. The wave retreated and left the room further away than it had been before, a warmth remained.

"Mate, you're not wrong about this," Leo said, slightly struggling with the words. "That taste, lemon, the spices, cool, what is that?"

"They flavor the water, put loads of stuff in to make it taste good, and cool the smoke," Tau said.

The wave came again. *Breathe in, hold, taste the lemon and the spices.* Leo held the smoke in his lungs until it felt like it was about to burn, then let it out. The smoke washed away every emotion, leaving a calm, blank beach. A desert island.

On Leo's third inhale, the room began to wobble. Distances changed, and noises became further away. The wave came and broke over Leo, the restaurant, Tau, and Allissa.

He glanced at Allissa. She was the reason he was here, his success. His victory. He felt a strange sense of pride.

Tau had been smoking for longer than Leo and Allissa, but Leo felt it affecting him already. He put the hose down. The first three drags had hit him so hard he didn't need any more. Leo still wanted to keep his head in the game.

Beside him, the eyes of the coal on top of the shisha pipe burned ferociously.

Leo glanced around the table and tried to think of something to say to the others. His tongue felt thick and the words didn't come. It felt as though the world had now reduced to the burning eyes of coal.

Leo felt the distant sting of anxiety, but now it was just a tiny flicker. Whatever was in the smoke had reduced that too. Leo longed to close his eyes and relax completely, but an instinct told him not to. He wanted to stay in the game.

His eye lids drooped as though each one weighed a ton.

Don't close your eyes.

Don't close your eyes.

Leo's eyes closed. Everything felt so good with his eyes closed.

Snapping back into consciousness, Leo forced his eyes open. He glanced around. The room waxed and waned, ebbed and flowed. It felt to Leo as though he were floating above the chair. He held on for everything he could.

Breathe in, and out.

The room spun and swayed across his vision.

He'd only had a couple of pulls on the smoke. Whatever was in there was super strong.

Leo tried to look at Tau across the table. Tau appeared as though in a dream, far away and moving further all the time. Tau's head rolled gently from side to side as though in control of itself.

Leo knew that in the real world he could reach out and touch Tau, but this didn't feel like the real world anymore. Distance and time were different here, and Leo didn't understand them.

Leo turned and saw Allissa struggling with the effects too. She stared into nothing, her jaw tensed and eyes wide.

No one was smoking anymore. The shisha hoses lay on the table.

Tau's head hung forwards. Having had more of the smoke and whatever it contained, he seemed completely out of it.

Leo tried to reach forward to tap one of Tau's arms which lay limp on the table. Tau seemed to move away. Tau was at the end of a tunnel. Everything else was darkness.

Time curved in on itself as Leo's movements slowed.

He needed to stay focused, or he knew he'd fall...

Breathe in, and out.

Breathe in, and out.

He needed to stay focused, or he knew he'd fall...

He needed to fight this.

Breathe in, and out. Breathe in, and out.

Every molecule of Leo's body wanted him to close his eyes and relax. Each individual atom told him to sleep. The space between atoms, the vibrations of energy between the subatomic particles which made up his body and all of time and space, told him to close his eyes and sleep.

But, he needed to stay focused.

He tried to focus on Tau's slumped figure. He strained to keep his eyes open.

He hoped Allissa was doing the same. Right now, he couldn't see her.

Then, through the fish-eyed tunnel vision which strained his brain, he noticed something. One of the waiters approached the table. Without a word, the waiter removed the coals and carried the shisha pipe back into the kitchen.

A moment passed — a sluggish, immeasurable, treacle-like moment.

Two waiters then appeared either side of Tau. With a hand under each of his arms, they raised Tau from the chair. Tau's slumped figure gave no resistance as the waiters lifted and then dragged him towards the kitchen door. Tau's limp feet trailed across the uneven ground.

Leo watched Tau and the waiters disappear in a haze. He tried to move, tried to stand, but the room was spinning. His legs were no longer beneath him.

Just concentrate on your breathing, he thought. *Don't close your eyes.*

Then the men came back and lifted Allissa. Her head rolled forward. She twisted, trying to put up a fight, but the effects of the drugs were too strong. The men dragged Allissa toward the kitchen.

The bad feeling which had gnawed at Leo's gut some minutes ago, came back full force. It hit him like a train at full speed. Suddenly, through the fog of the drugs, things made sense. They'd been set up to come here. They'd walked into a trap, wandered right into the jaws of death.

You have to move, thought Leo. The strength was rising in him.

You have to move.

You have to rescue Allissa and Tau.

Leo pulled together all his strength and somehow made it to his feet. He staggered towards the kitchen, moving as though he was wading through waist high water.

Leo picked his way across the restaurant. The walls seemed to bow and swirl around him. He focused just on the kitchen door ahead of him.

Finally, after an incredible effort, Leo reached the kitchen door. He supported himself on the doorframe. The walls of the restaurant danced as though taunting him.

The door hadn't shut, and a vertical bar of light seeped into the restaurant. Leo peered into the kitchen.

Allissa lay slumped in the arms of one of the waiters. Her head hung to the side. She muttered something, but Leo couldn't make out the words.

The waiters spoke in unrecognizable mutterings. One of the men picked up one of the serving dishes they had eaten from. He raised the dark, thick, heavy metal high in the air.

Leo recoiled with the movement. Leo had no doubt about what the man intended to do. Leo saw it happening in his mind's eye. Leo gasped for breath, but it felt as though the room contained no air.

The scene held, frozen in mid stride, before Leo's eyes.

Then, slowly at first, the waiter swung the dish down towards Allissa's skull.

28

Leo swallowed, shook himself into focus and shoved the door open.

Inside the kitchen, bright lights glared from overhead strips and steel counter-tops glimmered. Leo's footsteps pounded across the floor. Leo shouted something but didn't really know what it was.

The man holding Allissa's prone body looked up. The other man continued swinging the dish down towards her head.

Leo glanced at two half-prepared meals waiting on the counter. Leo snatched one of the dishes, sending meat and vegetables flying across the kitchen.

Allissa moaned, clearly coming around from the effects of the drugs.

Leo, his pulse roaring in his ears, leaped at the

waiter. He swung the dish high and smashed it into the man's shoulder. The man, with no hands free, couldn't block the strike. The waiter stumbled backwards. Leo's assault had the desired result, though. The dish the waiter held clanged harmlessly to the floor. Off balance, the waiter stumbled backwards and crashed into the counter.

Allissa made some gurgling noises. The sound of the commotion seemed to be pulling her from her stupor, that was good.

Leo attacked again, this time turning his attention to the man that held Allissa. The man dropped Allissa, and attempted to block Leo's assault. He didn't move in time. Leo socked the man hard on the side of the neck. Leo felt the shock vibrate up and down his arm as the waiter crumpled to the floor.

Allissa rolled across the floor, groaning.

Leo took a step back and spun to the left just in time to see the other man charge towards him. Leo swung the dish again, but this time he was too late.

The waiter caught the dish. His hands closed around the metal like a vice. The waiter pulled the dish from Leo's grip as though Leo was a naughty child. The waiter stepped forwards, his jaw set in an expression of menace. He threw the dish to the ground. The metal clanged hard several times against concrete.

Allissa groaned again. She was saying something, although Leo couldn't work out quite what it was.

Leo took two steps backwards. He felt the kitchen wall behind him. He couldn't go any further. With an explosive burst of energy, Leo pushed from the wall and shoved his opponent backwards. It felt like he was pushing against the trunk of a tree.

The waiter took a gentle step backwards but didn't lose his footing. This guy was clearly bigger than the other one. Leo grimaced. He glanced in panic around the kitchen, looking for something he could use as a weapon.

The waiter swung at Leo. Leo tried to move backwards, but the fist caught him in the ribs, sending him flying against a large fridge two feet away. Pain jarred through his body. Leo clenched his teeth and struggled upwards, sending several jars of spices rolling across the shelves and smashing to the floor.

Leo pulled himself up to his feet again. He locked eyes with the waiter. Without warning, the waiter lunged forward, his fist flying directly for Leo's face.

Fortunately, Leo saw the punch coming. He ducked and spun out of the way. He shoved the waiter with an elbow, causing him to misstep and stumble.

Leo darted to the right.

The waiter lunged again, this time sending a wild, wide punch towards Leo's face. Although this man was strong and powerful, Leo was beginning to realise his punches weren't all that accurate.

Leo spun to the side again, this time managing to grab a frying pan from the stove. He swung it his opponent's head.

The waiter blocked the attack with his forearm, but the force of the blow sent him back a step. He recovered quickly, grabbing a knife from the counter and lunging forward.

Leo scowled. The blade shone beneath the bright overhead lights.

The waiter lunged forward with the knife. The blade traced a line directly towards Leo's chest. At the last moment, Leo twisted out of the way. Leo gritted his teeth and tried to dart to the left, but there was nowhere to go. The waiter had trapped him in the kitchen's back corner.

Leo watched as the waiter approached. Was it really going to end like this? Dying in the kitchen of a backstreet restaurant really wasn't what Leo had imagined.

The waiter stepped forward again, the knifepoint steady in his hands. The waiter shoved Leo with his free hand. Leo stumbled backwards, hit the wall and then fell to the floor.

Leo noticed movement behind the waiter. Assuming it was the other man recovering from his fall, the last ounce of Leo's confidence drained.

Leo's fingers scratched against the wall, trying to lift himself up once more. Leo scrabbled backwards, right into the corner. He reached up to the counter, pushing another dish to the floor in the process. A thick cut of meat slammed to the floor with a wet slap.

The waiter stepped forwards, grinning.

Leo's heart slowed, treating every beat as though it was his last.

The knife came closer. Leo lifted his arms, a vain attempt to block his armed attacker.

Then, the waiter froze. The knife stopped for a second in midair and then slipped to the floor. The waiter's eyes rolled upwards and then right into the back of his head. He slumped to the floor.

Allissa stood behind the prone waiter, one of the dishes in her hands.

"Sorry I took a while," she said panting hard. "This stuff is strong."

Leo struggled to his feet, using the kitchen counters for support.

They both turned and darted across to Tau,

sprawled out on the floor. Leo placed a finger against his neck. Somewhere deep inside him, a pulse beat faintly.

"He's alive," Leo said, his voice coming out in short sharp bursts. "We need to get out of..."

"Leo, look, Leo... Hand..." Allissa's shrieking voice cut through the room like a blade.

Leo turned around and saw Allissa pointing at something on the floor. The object sat in the room's far corner.

Allissa tried to speak again, but the words didn't really make sense.

Leo struggled to his feet and looked at the thing in the corner of the kitchen. Leo blinked, not quite believing what he saw.

In the corner of the kitchen lay a human hand.

29

Four weeks until Mya's disappearance. Goa, India.

"How've you found your first traveling experience?" Mya asked. Nearly a month had passed since they had arrived in Mumbai. They had traveled north through the deserts and palaces of Rajasthan to the teeming hub of Delhi. From there, they had journeyed to Pushkar, Agra, and Varanasi for a trip down the swollen Ganges. Then they had boarded the train to Goa for five days of walking on the beach, gorging on fresh fish, and sipping late-night cocktails.

Leo lay back in the chair and gazed out at the white sand which looked like it could run on forever. Restaurants with big wicker chairs displayed the day's catch on tables of ice. Hawkers moved amongst the lounging tourists selling bangles, necklaces, or bits of string that promised to bring the wearer good luck.

"Hey, tall man."

"Where are you from?"

"Manchester United, yeah?" they shouted, starting conversations with anyone inexperienced enough not to ignore them.

Further up the beach, a herd of cows broke through the undergrowth and walked sedately between the chairs and tables. Tourists photographed the unique spectacle, impossible to imagine anywhere else in the world. The beasts dropped to the sand and warmed their backs in the fading sun.

"What has been your favorite part?" Mya asked.

"That's hard. It's all just been so good. Just been an incredible month," Leo said, swigging on a bottle of beer. "You know what? I think the last few days have been the best... Yeah. I loved seeing the Taj Mahal, and I loved the trip down the Ganges and all that, but there's just something incredible about being here. It's such a beautiful place."

A warm breeze pushed through the restaurant, causing the dark red cloth over a neighboring table to shiver. The gust brought with it the smell of sandal-wood and tropical undergrowth.

Kathmandu Killers

"It's been really special," Mya said. "I've always wanted to come to India. Are you ready to go home?"

"Home feels so far away right now," Leo answered.

"Yeah, but do you want to go back there?" Mya pushed.

"No, I don't think so. We've been away so long, this sort of feels like our lives now," Leo said, watching Mya as though entranced by her. She really was beautiful. Her dark hair had grown in the last month, and she had taken to tying it up with garish headbands bought at local markets. Her skin glowed, boasting the tan of the last month, causing her eyes and teeth to shine extra brightly.

"Yeah, that's what I feel too," Mya said. She reached across the table and took Leo's hand.

"Where would you like to go now, if you could?" Leo asked.

Mya thought about it for an instant, looking out to sea. "I'd go down to Vietnam, then across to Thailand. There are loads of places I've always wanted to see there. More temples. Beautiful food. The islands. From there, I'd go across to China, starting in Hong Kong."

Leo noticed the reflection of the setting sun in her eyes. The moment was perfect.

Leo's words deserted him, and his breath drew

tight. He felt panic rising within him, but at the same time, he felt exhilarated and invigorated. He took a deep breath and held it in. This was his moment. Their moment.

"There's something I'd like to say to you," he said, holding his nerve.

"There's something I need to tell you too. Can I go first?" Mya said, turning to look at him.

Leo swallowed and nodded.

"I might as well just say it. I've wanted to tell you for a few days, but haven't found the moment." Mya glanced at their interlocked hands.

Leo's mind roamed, wondering what she was about to say.

"We're not going home tomorrow," Mya said.

"What do you mean?"

"You know how we were going to come here for two months and travel on to Vietnam afterwards? But you couldn't get the time off work," Mya said.

"Yeah,"

"Well, I knew you'd like it so much, and you'd want to carry on, so even though you said no, I booked it."

Silence fell over the couple. The sun continued its labored descent toward the Indian Ocean. Leo didn't know what to say or think. He stared open mouthed at Mya.

"Hold on. Let me get this right," he said, finally finding his voice. He shook his hand free from Mya's and crossed his arms. "We're booked to go somewhere else tomorrow? Not home?"

"Yes. I've booked it all. We fly to Hanoi, then we're going to travel down to Ho Chi Minh City and then fly across to Thailand for five days on a beautiful island. Then, after that, we go home."

Words alluded Leo. His mind spun. How had Mya done this without telling him? She'd lied to him, for months.

"You didn't know how much things cost anyway," Mya said, sensing his confusion. "So I just told you it was the amount for two months when I booked it."

"But... but... I'm supposed to go back to work in three days," Leo stuttered.

"I know. But ultimately, Leo, that place has treated you so badly. They never give you the opportunities you deserve. They work you so hard for rubbish money. You deserve more."

There was an element of truth in what she said, Leo knew that, but it also sounded like an insult. Mya had lied to him. The woman he loved, the woman he wanted to marry, had lied to him. Leo hated the thought of her deceiving him. The thought of them traveling all this way and spending all this time together while she was holding this secret tore at his heart.

Mya watched Leo, challenging him to argue. He had nothing more to say.

"I'm sorry for lying to you. I just knew that once you were here you wouldn't want to go home. I was right, too."

"That's not the point!" Leo's anger rose. "You can't just do that. You can't always have it your way. I said I could only do a month. You should have respected that. I know you don't like my job, I get that, you've said that before. But that's my choice to make." Leo looked at the ocean, not wanting to meet her eye.

"I'm going for a walk," Leo said, spitting out the words. "On my own."

ONE OF THE waiter's mumbled and moved about on the floor, snapping Leo and Allissa back into the present.

"We need to get out of here, now," Leo said.

"How's he?" Allissa pointed at Tau, her voice soft.

"Alive. Still out of it, though. They were obviously planning on dealing with us first."

Leo swallowed, trying to extinguish the bile which

bubbled in his stomach. He stepped across to Tau and lifted him from the floor. Allissa moved around to Tau's other arm.

Tau groaned with the movement. Fortunately, when Leo and Allissa had him standing up, his feet started moving across the floor as though walking by instinct. Leo and Allissa half-dragged, half carried Tau through the door and out into the empty restaurant. They pushed through the door, shoving chairs and tables out of the way. The kitchen door swung closed behind them. They reached the restaurant's main door and slipped out into the alleyway. Before the door closed, Leo heard movement and voices in the kitchen behind them. A muffled voice spoke and then another answered.

"We need to move," Leo said, upping his pace. "They'll be coming soon."

The voices came again, louder this time.

Leo focused on putting his feet on solid ground, dragging Tau with them. Within a few paces, they were walking at a good speed. Leo straightened up and pumped his legs as hard as possible. His ribs ached from the brawl with the waiter.

They reached the end of the alleyway, all running as best they could. Something clattered behind them and voices shouted unknown words.

Leo and Allissa didn't stop to look. They powered on, dodging piles of rubbish where they could, crashing through them when they couldn't. Leo had no idea where they were going. They turned right at a crossroads, then left, then right again.

Leo ran until his legs felt like knives. He ran until he tasted acid in his mouth. Then he ran some more.

Tau mumbled something garbled and twisted his head this way and that.

They charged into another street, darker than the last. It was just another dusty alleyway lit by the occasional flickering light.

Leo thought about their pursuers but refused to turn and see how close they were. Stopping and turning now would waste valuable seconds.

They made a couple more turns and Leo lost all track of how long they'd been running.

Finally, Leo saw a light ahead. The narrow street joined another. This street was still gloomy, but the dim streetlights looked like a beacon to eyes used to the darkness. Leo and Allissa sped up, running towards the light like moths.

The road was large by Kathmandu's standards. The closed shutters of shops lined both sides. Like the rest of the sleeping city, the street was empty and quiet.

Leo and Allissa moved around a parked car and continued half-running, half-dragging Tau.

Leo's vision fizzed. The road waned and jolted with each step. Twice he fell into the metal shutters of the closed shops and crashed to the floor.

They stumbled against a pink and white taxi. Something stirred inside the small vehicle.

Leo stopped in his tracks. Allissa almost stumbled, letting go of Tau.

Leo took Tau's weight and peered through the taxi's rear window. A man lay curled up beneath a blanket on the backseat of the tiny vehicle. Leo banged on the glass. The man pulled the blanket up over his head.

Allissa dug a wad of notes from a pocket and pressed them against the window.

The taxi driver glanced up. Noticing the money, he climbed forward and unlocked the doors.

Leo yanked open the back door of the taxi, pushed Tau in, and then climbed inside himself.

"The airport," Leo instructed impetuously. "We're getting out of here, right now."

The taxi pulled away, picking up speed on the empty road.

Leo turned and looked at the passage from which they'd emerged. Leo thought about the restaurant and the countless other people who hadn't made it out of that place alive.

Leo peered out of the taxi as the buildings merged into a blur of colors and shapes. Leo heard voices, but right now, he didn't care. He was warm and comfortable and alive.

As the taxi rumbled and shook, Leo glanced at Allissa.

"Where are we going?" Tau mumbled, crammed in the central seat. "What's going on?"

"Nice of you to wake up," Allissa said. "How you feeling?"

"Awful," Tau said. He touched the back of his head. "Did someone punch me?"

"Yeah. It could have been a whole lot worse, though," Leo said. "Do you think we should take him to a hospital?"

Allissa looked at the bump on the back of Tau's head. "I think he's in much more danger if we stay here. We need to get out of the city as soon as we can. We'll keep checking on him and get him looked at tomorrow if needed."

No one said anything for a few long seconds. Leo noticed the taxi driver peering at them inquisitively in the rear-view mirror.

"Big night," Leo said, nodding at Tau. "Some

people just can't handle their drink.

"Sorry if this is stating the obvious," Allissa said. "But it was no accident we turned up there, was it?"

"Absolutely not. That was set up from the start. I think it's partly my fault."

"How was that your fault?" Alissa said, her mind still foggy from the effects of the drugs. "You just followed that guy, along with everyone else."

"Yeah. That guy who showed us to the restaurant and then disappeared before it got nasty. He knew exactly what was coming."

Leo watched the city stream past the windows, self-doubt circling his mind.

"I should have seen that coming. I don't know how, but I should have seen that coming," Leo said. He looked at Allissa. Finding her had been his success. He'd done it. Only for it to go so badly wrong.

"How could you have predicted that?" Alissa asked, turning to face Leo. They locked eyes. Allissa's gaze was now as clear as it had been before smoking whatever was in that pipe.

"It's horrible to say this." Leo stuttered over his words. "But I think your father set that up."

The color drained from Allissa's face. She tried to argue, but couldn't find the words.

It just all made a horrible sort of sense.

Almost an hour later, after three stops to gather their things, Leo, Allissa, and Tau arrived outside the airport. Beneath thick clouds, dawn was coming. At almost the exact moment that the taxi stopped, raindrops the size of bullets began hammering against the roof. Leo jumped out and peered at the sky. A bolt of lightning flashed somewhere across the heavens. They grabbed their bags from the trunk and ran, hunched over, into the terminal.

Inside, the airport terminal smelled of lemon and damp. The building was a mid-twentieth century reminder of what the city was trying to be. Despite the early hour, the terminal teemed with people all wanting to leave the city. Leo soon realized that was because they were all waiting for flights that were either delayed or cancelled. Some people sat bright and optimistic, chatting on benches or together on the floor. These were the experienced travelers. To people like this, the delay represented just another story from the road. *The harder it is to get there, the better it'll be when we do.*

Wind and rain slashed against the windows. Lightening swirled around the skies.

Leo, Allissa and Tau pushed their way towards one of the departure desks. Leo intended to get them all on the first flight out of the city, regardless of its destination. From there they would rest and work out what to do next. They waited in line for several minutes, Leo impatiently glancing around for any sign of their foe.

Finally, they reached the front of the line and Leo explained what they needed.

"No flights leaving for at least the next twenty-four-hours," the clerk replied, not even looking up from his screen.

"What do you mean there are no flights?" Leo said, his voice raised over the hubbub of the terminal.

"I'm sorry." The man looked up at Leo. The dark rings circling his eyes showed that he was having a long night too. "All flights are canceled until the storm passes." He tapped at the computer. "I can get you booked on one to Delhi tomorrow afternoon, but that's the earliest, I'm afraid."

"We need to get out of here now," Leo said.

"You're not the only person waiting, sir," the man said, devoid of all energy. "Do want those seats or not?"

"We need to get out of here sooner than that. This can't be happening." Leo groaned, feeling the tightness in his chest return. His breathing became short, sharp snatches of air.

"If you want to get anywhere quicker than that, then you'll have to get the bus to Pokhara. Flights are still leaving from there. The bus still goes even in bad weather."

Leo gasped a breath, but barely felt its relief.

"Thank you, we'll do that," Allissa said. She put her arm on Leo's shoulder and led him away from the departures desk. The line of frustrated travelers shuffled forwards.

Allissa led them to a bench between a sign advertising flights to the Himalayas and a humming vending machine stripped of its contents. Most of the space sat in darkness, the lights that did work flashed like the sky outside.

"This happens sometimes," Tau said, slumping down into the seat. It seemed that even he was coming around now. "The whole city shuts down in bad weather. You're at the mercy of the mountains here."

Leo gazed out through the glass. Rain beat ferociously against the aircraft-free tarmac. Clearly the airliners had left before the storm and the smaller planes had been moved to their hangars. Maybe the expected storm was that ferocious that even being exposed on the ground could cause serious damage to planes.

Leo placed his head in his hands, his mind swirling and pounding like the storm outside.

He needed to go. He needed to get out of this city.

He wasn't the sort of person who could do this. Coming here had been a terrible idea.

THE DAY of Mya's disappearance. Koh Tao, Thailand.

"I don't think I've ever been anywhere as beautiful as this." Leo gazed up at the sky as the color drained. The noise of the island swelled. Birds flashed through the twilight streaks of pink and purple.

"I knew you'd like it," Mya replied in a whisper, her feet kicking the water which lapped beneath the jetty.

"How did we get here? I mean, this is crazy, like it's a different world," Leo said, pointing towards the inky ocean in front of them. They'd been traveling for two months, but this was the first time he'd seen an ocean like this.

A bird squawked and a boat crept across the horizon.

"Koh Tao's a special place because it's hard to get to. When things are hard to find, that's when they're precious," Mya said, looking out into nothing. Her hands gripped the side of the jetty and her feet swung freely. She was beautiful. Her smile was currency across the world.

"I'm just glad to be here... with you," Leo said,

looking at her profile in the light of the setting sun. "Even the extra month. I'm so happy to be here."

This was the time, he knew it, tonight. He had kept the ring hidden in his wallet for over a month now, waiting for tonight. This time, this place, this woman.

Mya turned to face Leo as he lay back on the jetty. Water slapped the supports beneath the platform. Somewhere nearby, people spoke in an unfathomable language.

"I knew you'd like it," Mya said.

"Yeah. I'm struggling to take it in. I've never been anywhere as beautiful as this." Leo rested up on his elbows, attempting to look relaxed. Inside his chest a storm of anxiety raged.

Now would be the perfect moment.

Mya leaned forward.

"To be... to be here with you is so special," Leo said as Mya turned to look at him. "And we... I mean 'I', I hadn't even planned to come here."

"Yeah, it's been great," Mya said, turning back to the water. A chill passed across her body, blowing her loose-fitting top tight against her profile.

Leo's eyes followed; he couldn't help it. He turned and fumbled the ring from his wallet. The one-kneed stance that tradition dictated wasn't possible on the jetty, but Leo hoped the setting and moment would make up for it. He wanted this to be perfect. It would be perfect.

Leo took a deep breath. The air tasted of salt, tamarind, lime, of love, hope, and opportunity. It was a scent that he'd remember for years to come. He exhaled.

"Will you marry me?" He blurted the words, spitting them out.

An eddy of wind skipped past, rushing towards the curving palm trees on the shoreline. The bay shivered. Time hung in the balance. Leo held his breath, unblinking.

"I..." Mya stalled, following a train of thought but cutting it before it started. She looked from Leo's expectant expression to the ring in his hands.

"Oh my gosh, that's so beautiful." She plucked it from his fingers. Mya held up the ring. Its colors refracted in the twilight.

"Come to our room in five minutes," she said, climbing to her feet. "Then you'll get your answer."

Mya stood, turned, and walked toward the beach.

Leo settled back on his elbows, stared at the bruised horizon, and tried to ignore the bitter sting of disappointment.

That was so typical of Mya, doing things her way.

30

Leo wanted to leave, yet the mountain city wasn't finished with him. The weather had closed in. No planes would be leaving for a while.

Leo climbed to his feet and together they picked their way back through the terminal. Tau, now back to his normal ebullient self, hailed a cab. The car screeched to a stop, rain hammering against the roof like angry fists.

They stashed their bags in the trunk and climbed in. Leo noticed another car crawl past. Its bright lights swept by, illuminating the raindrops. Leo watched suspiciously until the car disappeared in the gloom. Everything in this city felt dangerous and unsettling now.

Inside the car, Tau explained to the driver what

they needed. They would employ the driver for the next two days. That's how long it would take to get to Pokhara, and for him to drive back to Kathmandu. A price was quickly negotiated and the driver agreed. They set off, swishing through the water.

Leo thought he should feel some kind of shock after the events of the day. He'd never seen that sort of violence, let alone caused it. The memories swirled uselessly in his mind. Again and again, he felt the cold dish in his sweating palms. Again and again, he sensed the jarring vibrations as the metal arched through the air and struck the man on the neck. Again and again, he saw the waiter fold to the floor, not knowing if he'd injured or even killed the man.

"You did the right thing," Allissa said, as though reading his thoughts. "I would have done the same."

"I can't stop thinking about it," Leo replied. "Feeling the jolt. I know it was the right thing to do. I know he killed people. But... well, I don't want him to be dead."

"He won't be, I'm sure," Allissa said, turning from the window. In silhouette, Allissa's expression was neither a smile nor a frown. Their eyes connected until Leo looked down at his hands.

"I think my father underestimated you," Allissa

said, reaching over and taking Leo's hand. "And I'm very glad he did."

The road from Kathmandu to Pokhara is well-traveled but treacherous. The dusty surface snakes across mountains, down valleys and through forests. Many times, it clings precariously to the side of cliffs with nothing to break the deadly fall.

Fortunately for Allissa, Tau and Leo, the road was quiet this early in the morning. Bloated trucks lay dormant in any available space, their windscreens covered to give the sleeping drivers some privacy. They would start their plodding journey again when light and weather permitted.

It was unusual to make the journey during adverse weather. The unpredictable road was dangerous enough in good weather. With perilous drops and sharp bends, traveling during the storm was not much short of madness. But for Leo and the others, it was essential.

"I have to say, I'm very sorry for getting in such a state back there," Tau said, turning around in the passenger seat. "I've had that shisha smoke many times before but that..."

"That was something very different indeed," Allissa said. "That's obviously how they get unsuspecting customers back into the kitchen."

"There's no knowing how many people they had back in that kitchen," Leo muttered, feeling his stomach lurch. They had eaten in that restaurant. He tried to suppress the feeling, but it wouldn't go.

"Stop the car," Leo shouted.

The taxi screeched to a halt. Leo leapt out and emptied his stomach in a drainage ditch. The rain pounded down on him as he purged the meat they'd eaten back at the restaurant. Human meat. Leo wandered back to the taxi, soaked through, but feeling a little less grim.

The driver and Tau exchanged some words. Tau opened the glove box and found a few cans of soda. He passed one to Leo.

Leo snapped the can open and gulped down half the contents. Although sodden to the skin, he felt a little bit better already.

The city rolled past silently for the next half an hour. Dark windows were closed to the outside world as hardworking residents battened down against the rain. Areas of gloom between illuminated buildings grew and grew, until Leo looked out on nothing but the grey morning. Soon, the taxi's dim yellow headlights were alone in the night.

The driver dropped down a gear and accelerated toward a hill. He was still driving as though they were swarming through the city. Tau reassured him that they didn't need to rush. At first the driver didn't seem to understand, then he laid off the pressure, sat back slightly, and fell into a more sedentary pace. The engine even calmed from its usual scream of protest to a compliant, productive hum.

In the back, Leo and Allissa sat alert, looking frequently out the rear window. The lights of the city, which had drawn their attention, had been replaced by the murky dawn light and lashing ran. Occasionally the lights of passing cars dazzled them as they sloshed through the rain.

After an hour, the driver slowed as they pulled through a collection of houses. Tau, who himself was losing focus as the exhaustion of the day caught up on him, asked what was happening.

"Fuel," the driver said, tapping the gauge on the display which crept toward empty. "Not many stopping places on the road ahead."

The bright lights of the fuel station flooded into the car. The taxi pulled alongside the pumps, their analogue dials showing a row of zeros.

The driver got out and walked across the forecourt to a small cabin and spoke in through an open window. Switching on the pump looked like more of a complex transaction than it might be in Europe, Leo thought.

Tau climbed out and took the opportunity to stretch.

Leo followed. It felt good to be out of the cramped car. He pushed his arms skyward and straightened his legs. Allissa did the same, rubbing her eyes. Sheets of rain hammered down on the fueling station's canopy, obscuring the outside world with watery curtains.

Leo inhaled a deep breath of the cool, fresh morning air. The smell here was different. The wet jungle mingled with the spice of local cooking and burning incense. It smelt different, as though they'd finally left the city behind. Leo's muscles relaxed and his mind calmed.

Leo stretched again, tilting his head backwards and pushing his shoulder blades together while looking at the sky. Gone was the orange glow of the city.

A Jeep drove into the petrol station behind their taxi. Its harsh lights cast long shadows, scanning the jungle, the cabin, and dazzling Leo. The engine stuttered to a halt, and the lights died. The silence thickened.

Leo didn't think anything of it until he saw Tau tense.

One man climbed out of the Jeep, followed by a second. The vehicle's suspension creaked.

Leo experienced that prickling sensation on the back of his neck which usually meant something bad was about to happen. Something really bad.

He turned around slowly and looked at the men. One had a bruise forming on his neck, the other a swollen lump on his head. Both carried long, glinting, knives. The men took a step forwards, fanning out to block Leo and Allissa's movement.

A roaring sound started in Leo's chest, then moved up his throat and into his head. It took him most of a heartbeat to realize it was his own voice.

"Get back in the car!" Leo shouted. "Get back in the car, now!"

Tau swung around and saw the men. His eyes nearly swelled from their sockets.

Tau, beside the front passenger's door, leapt into the car and scrambled across into the driver's seat. Allissa was next in, slipping into the back and slamming the door. Leo jumped in last, although he was a moment too late. As he swung the door closed, a strong hand seized it. The door was swung open, jarring on its hinges. One of the men appeared in the door, just inches from Leo's face. The knife flashed as it moved. Leo twisted out of the way, ending up in

Allissa lap. The knife swung a tenth of an inch past his face and slammed into the seat.

Fortunately, the taxi driver had left the keys in the ignition. Tau started the engine. The taxi stuttered to life, the engine only catching on the third of forth rotation. It wasn't reassuring.

The man on Allissa's side of the car attempted to pull the door open. A moment before he was able to, Allissa pushed down on the locking lever. Frustrated, the man battered at the glass with the butt of the knife.

The man on Leo's side of the car, pulled back, removing the knife from the seat. He prepared for another strike, and this time Leo didn't think he would miss. Leo swung around, lifting his legs out of the footwell, and slamming them both into the man's groin. It was a solid strike and doubled the man over.

Tau finally managed to get the recalcitrant gearbox engaged and stamped down on the gas. Thin tires spun across the gravel, sending the car into a slide. The tires finally found traction and they lurched forwards. The car shot out from beneath the canopy. Water poured across the windscreen, obscuring everything. Tau bashed frantically at the controls, eventually finding the wipers.

The man on Leo's side of the car recovered and

lurched forwards, attempting to grab on to the car as it pulled away. The car slid out of his reach just in time. The door swung closed and clicked into place. The man fell, sprawled out across the road in the car's wake, earning a face-full of dust and rain for his efforts.

A crash on Allissa's side of the taxi drew Leo's attention. The other waiter clung on to the taxi's roof rack. Leo turned and saw the man grimace in concentration through the rear windscreen.

The waiter struck the glass several times with the butt of the knife. A spider's web of cracks covered the glass.

"We've got company!" Allissa said.

Tau glanced in the rear-view mirror and then muttered a string of expletives in several of the languages he spoke. Tau swung the car hard to the left, almost touching the rock-wall that towered over them on the mountain side of the road. Then he swung them to the right, just inches from the flimsy barrier which was their only protection from the perilous drop. Leo, for one, was really glad he couldn't see how far the drop went.

The man, his fingers losing all color, managed to maintain his grip

"It's the roof rack," Leo said. "He's holding on to the roof rack."

Leo scrambled through the car and into the passenger seat.

Tau took another curve as quickly as possible. The feeble barrier slid treacherously close to the taxi. They splashed through a giant puddle of mud-colored water.

Leo slid down the passenger's window and stuck his head out. Sure enough, the waiter was holding on to the roof rack with one hand, while battering against the glass with the other. With each strike, the glass bowed. It wouldn't be long before he broke through it completely.

Leo turned his attention to the roof rack. The thing was attached to the roof with four clamps. Leo leaned forwards and undid the clamp at the rear. Preoccupied with smashing through the window, the waiter didn't notice. The bolt undid easily, and when it was loose, the clamp rattled against the roof.

Another strike shook the rear window. Shards of glass sailed through the car. The man had made a hole of about three inches across in the rear window. He stuck the blade through but the hole wasn't yet big enough for his arm.

Leo turned his attention to the roof rack clamp at

the front. He undid the bolt and the clamp released. The roof rack shook against the roof now.

The waiter looked up just in time to see Leo pull the clamp from its housing.

"I've got the wheel," Leo said, ducking back inside taking the steering wheel from Tau. Fortunately, the road straightened out for a few hundred feet. His feet still on the pedals, Tau wound down the window, he found the clamp and twisted the bolt. Now with three clamps loose the roof rack shuddered against metal. Inside the car it sounded as though the thing was fighting for freedom. Tau took the wheel again and Leo slid back over to the window. He nodded to Allissa who slid down her window and prepared to tackle the final clamp.

Leo put his head out through the window and stood up. Wind and rain howled around his ears, deafening him. His hair flapped uncontrollably.

"Hey! Over here!" Leo shouted, shaking the roof rack. It was now wobbly, rising and falling with each bump in the road.

The waiter looked up, a snarl of unconcealed madness on his face.

Leo saw Allissa's hand snake through the window and twist the bolt. It only took one turn and Leo felt the whole thing disconnect from the car.

Leo grinned down at the man. The waiter, crouched on the rear of the car, snarled up at Leo.

"See ya!" Leo said, heaving up on the roof rack with all his might. The metal lifted. For a moment it looked as though it might come tumbling back down again. Then, as though being dragged by an invisible hand, the roof rack shot backwards, spinning, and tumbling in the air.

The waiter let go of the roof rack and leapt. Fortunately for him, Tau had slowed the taxi for an upcoming corner. He hit the asphalt and dropped into a roll.

The roof rack fared less well, shattering on impact into nothing more than a pile of twisted metal.

Leo saw a pair of headlights approach from behind.

Tau slowed the taxi further.

The following car stopped. The other waiter climbed out and helped his partner up. The man climbed with a limp but seemed to have made the fall surprisingly unscathed.

Leo saw the waiter hobble towards their car. Then the taxi rounded a bend and their foe disappeared from view,

31

"It's not over yet," Leo said, sliding back into the passenger seat and raising the window. Even with the window closed, his ears buzzed. "Are you okay?" he said, turning to Allissa.

"Yes, thanks to you," Allissa said, brushing shattered glass from her clothes.

"I'm fine too, thanks for asking," Tau said, grinning.

"You always are," Leo replied, nudging Tau gently in the side.

A pair of headlights pierced the night behind them. The other car was approaching, fast. Leo glanced at the barrier, a constant reminder of the danger that lurked around every corner.

Tau approached another corner as quickly as he dared. The tires screeched and for a moment it felt as though the car was just going to slide straight off the edge.

Despite Tau's efforts, the pursuing Jeep started to close the distance. The waiters were clearly driving a more appropriate vehicle. It was also clear that they were determined to finish what they'd started, no matter what it took.

Leo wondered how much Stockwell was paying them. He felt a ball of rage solidify in his stomach. Whatever it took him, Stockwell wouldn't get away with this.

Tau gritted his teeth and gripped the steering wheel. The taxi's engine whined like a beast in agony. It felt as though it was moments away from conking out altogether.

The men in the Jeep closed the gap further still, their headlights shining bright in the taxi's rear-view mirror.

Leo thought through their options. The taxi was low on fuel, in a less powerful car, on one of the world's most dangerous roads. They couldn't outrun the men forever, and a crash on this road in this weather, would be nothing short of fatal.

Suddenly, he saw a narrow track branching off to

the left. It was barely visible in the darkness, but Leo knew it may be their only chance.

"That way," he shouted. "Up there!"

Tau flung the taxi into a slide. The wheels locked and the car barreled around the curve, just making the turning before they collided with a vast wall of rock.

Tau accelerated hard up the unpaved track. Little more than a footpath, the taxi flung grit, stones and chunks of wet mud in all directions. Tau pushed the car as fast as he could, the front sliding wildly from left to right. Tau fought with the steering wheel to bring them back to the center of the track.

"They're still following us," Allissa said, her voice grave.

Leo peered through the rear window. In a smaller vehicle and with Tau's near-crazy driving, the taxi's lead had increased, but the Jeep still followed.

The sound of the tires slapping wet earth changed. Now the grit skittered rather than squelched. Leo peered out at the sky and saw traces of blue through the clouds.

"We've moved above the storm," Tau said. "We're up in the mountains now. See the ground and plants aren't even wet."

Tau was right, everything here was miraculously

dry and bright. It was as though they'd turned from rain to shine in the flick of a switch.

The track narrowed further, branches whipping at the windscreen. From the passenger seat, Leo could hardly see anything of the route ahead. He wondered whether, with a growing sense of dread, if this hadn't been such a good idea.

Then, suddenly, the track opened into a wide and level plateau. The ground beneath the wheels became firm too. They were now driving over solid rock.

Looking through the windscreen, Leo noticed a moment too late what they were heading towards. In the taxi's weak lights, he saw the ground drop out of sight. It took him a moment to realize what that meant. He pointed wildly through the windscreen. They were heading, full throttle, for a ravine.

"Stop!" Leo shouted, his hands hitting the dash. "Stop now!"

Tau saw the drop at about the same time and applied the brake. He swung the wheel hard to the left, sending the car into a spin. Leo looked out of the window on his side as the perilous drop neared. The taxi rumbled closer and closer. For what felt like a really long time it looked as though they were just going to fly straight over the precipice. But finally, thankfully, the taxi slowed. Leo slid across the seat and crashed against the glass. Rubber screamed against rock. The whole taxi shook. Then, eventually, all became still.

Looking out through the window, Leo struggled for breath. He had never before literally seen his life flash before his eyes. He struggled out of the car, his heart beating ferociously in his throat. Fifteen feet away, the ground ended and dropped away. Leo turned his back to the abyss. He really didn't want to see how far down they might have fallen.

"That way," Tau said, pointing across the ravine. Twenty feet from the car, a rope bridge hung from one cliff to the other. As Leo had suspected, the path was really one for the thousands of hikers that visited this part of Nepal each year.

Tau started in the direction of the rope bridge.

"No wait!" Leo shouted, hearing the distant rumble of the approaching Jeep. The men, it seemed, were taking their time. Like a cat playing with their prey, they were going to make this last.

"That's exactly what they'd expect us to do. This way." Leo pointed off into the jungle.

"I really think we should," Tau pointed across the bridge.

"Trust me," Leo said. "I've seen enough Indiana Jones films to know that rope bridges are always a bad idea."

"Always," Allissa agreed, nodding.

Outnumbered, Tau conceded and the three of them ran into the jungle. They'd only just concealed themselves behind a bush when the Jeep rumbled on to the plateau.

Driving a lot more carefully that Tau had been, the Jeep slowed gently and then stopped beside the taxi. The men got out and did a three sixty of the area. For an awful moment Leo thought that some footprints or broken branches might just give their location away. The men turned back towards the taxi. They pointed at the rope bridge.

"It's working," Allissa hissed, surprisingly close beside Leo.

The men walked towards the rope bridge. One of them staggered, clearly still in pain after his fall from the car.

They paused at the bridge's entrance. The injured man said something, and the other replied.

"Come on," Leo hissed. "Just get over there."

As though hearing Leo's commands, the men stepped on to the bridge. The whole structure swung as the men staggered their way across. Although Leo wasn't particularly scared of heights, crossing such a construction wasn't something he longed to do. He thought about the ravine several hundred feet beneath the men.

"Anyone got a knife?" Leo said.

Allissa shook her head.

"No," Tau said. "But I have got this." He pulled out a fancy-looking silver cigarette lighter.

"Hold on a minute, did you take that from..."

"Miles, yeah! The guy was such a show off, I thought I'd relieve him of it. In the end he stitched us up, so it was some weird kind of justice."

"Worth an arm and a leg," Allissa quipped, mimicking the Australian's accent.

"Can't argue with that." Leo took the lighter and pushed out through the trees.

The men had dipped out of sight inside the ravine. That meant they must be about half way across the bridge, Leo thought.

Leo held his finger to his lips as he, Tau and Allissa approached.

As the men started to climb up the other side, towards the opposite cliff, Leo struck the lighter. A flame danced from the top. He quickly set fire to all the ropes connecting the bridge to their side of the ravine. When the ropes were burning well, he passed the lighter back to Tau.

"Hey fellas!" Leo shouted, cupping his hands around his mouth.

The men froze. The bridge continued to wobble for a few seconds before falling still. The men turned around slowly, clearly realizing their error.

Leo pointed at the burning ropes. "You've got a decision to make. I'd say these ropes have got about twenty seconds before they split. I would definitely suggest you're not on the bridge when that happens."

The man in front turned around and tried to force his way backwards, the other man tried to force his way forwards to the closer side. They shouted at each other.

"Well, that's not going to work, is it?" Leo said. "You've got fifteen seconds now."

The men argued. The bridge beneath them groaned and shook. Hearing the noise, the man at the front decided safety was better than revenge and together they hurried up to the other side of the ravine.

One of the ropes burned through, sending a shudder through the whole structure. The men hurried on, almost climbing over one another.

"Quickly now!" Allissa shouted, when the men were still six feet from the other side.

Another rope snapped, whipping down into the ravine like a mad, fiery snake. The bridge hung at an angle. The first man scrambled on to the opposite cliff just in time. He dropped to his stomach and pulled the other man up.

The third, then the fourth rope snapped, sending the bridge falling against the opposite cliff. The men lay, panting for a few seconds. Recovering, they climbed to their feet and stared across at Leo with fire in their eyes.

"For what it's worth," Leo said. "I think you made the right decision."

One of the men shouted across the ravine.

"You don't want to know what he's saying about you," Tau said.

Leo and Allissa turned back towards the vehicles. "He can say whatever he wants," Leo said.

Passing the Jeep, Allissa peered inside. "Wait a minute," she said, climbing into the driver's seat. The keys were still in the ignition. She started the engine. "Now this is a bit more comfortable."

Now the men shouted even more aggressively. Allissa waved at them through the window.

"We should probably take this back to the driver, though," Tau said, pointing at the taxi.

"That's absolutely the right thing to do," Leo said. "But I'm definitely riding in here," he pointed towards the Jeep.

Together, to the sound of shouted Nepali expletives, the two vehicles set off back towards the road.

32

Driving the Jeep back towards the fueling station, the events of the evening started to work through Allissa's mind.

Weirdly, she thought of those crime documentaries where the shocked neighbors always commented that the person next door seemed so normal. That was until they were found to have fifty dead bodies in the basement.

For her, it wasn't like that at all. She could picture it all in graphic detail. She could imagine her father's chubby fingers dialing the call to order her murder. She could visualize his rolls of flesh wobbling as instructions were given and his sweaty brow wiped ceremoniously after hanging up the phone. Her only disappointment was that she hadn't worked it out for herself.

What surprised Allissa the most, perhaps, was that she didn't feel anything about it, yet. She thought that maybe she should feel shocked, or horrified, or scared, or surprised, or useless. But she just felt nothing. She felt empty.

Almost thirty minutes later the small convoy arrived back at the fueling station. The taxi driver walked over from the cabin, as though having his car stolen was the most normal thing in the world.

"We will pay for any damage," Leo said, climbing out of the Jeep. "You'll need a new roof rack and a new rear windscreen, that's for sure."

The driver wobbled his head from side to side and then strolled over to the fuel pump. The pump shuddered to life, protesting the arduous task with a series of knocks and bangs. The canopy's lights dimmed and flickered with the strain on the electric current. When the fueling was done, the driver turned and spoke to Tau. He spoke in Nepalese but made an effort to use the English words he knew.

Allissa and Leo listened intently.

Leo heard the word "home" used several times.

Tau turned to translate.

"Horan — he indicated the taxi driver — "says his family home is nearby, an hour farther down this road. He suggests that we stop for a few hours and get some rest, that is if you still want him to take us to Pokhara."

Leo and Allissa glanced at each other. "Absolutely we still want to go to Pokhara," Allissa said. "And yes, breaking the journey sounds good.

"They'll have food, and somewhere we can sleep," Tau said. "We'll continue tomorrow."

An hour later, following in the Jeep, Leo and Allissa saw the taxi slow and turn up a narrow farm track.

"I hope it's not like the last track we went up," Leo muttered.

Fortunately, it wasn't. This track went up a steep incline and then wound between a collection of buildings. The taxi stopped. Allissa pulled up alongside and switched off the engine too. There was no sound, other than the murmur of insects and the whisper of wind through the trees.

Horan beckoned them to follow.

"This is where his family lives," Tau translated.

Horan walked up the hill, avoiding plants, trees, and uneven ground. The others followed his quick footsteps.

They reached the building, and Horan pushed

Kathmandu Killers

open the door. Instinctively, he found a switch and warm light swamped them.

The room was comfortable. A light dampened by a wicker shade hung in the middle, and three wicker chairs surrounded a table.

Horan shouted a greeting. A young woman appeared from a door at the back, squinting against the light. Her face brightened when she saw Horan, and she rushed across the room to greet him. She looped her arms around his thin neck and pulled him close. When she noticed the others, she straightened her posture and smiled. An older man and woman followed from a different door wearing the same bleary expressions. They too brightened as they welcomed Horan home. Horan introduced them one by one and Tau translated for Leo and Allissa.

"This is Horan's mother, father, and wife. He says we should sit. He will find us something to drink and eat."

Allissa and Leo sat awkwardly on one of the wicker chairs, feeling like intruders.

Horan's wife woke the children and brought them from the bedroom to see their father. They rubbed their eyes with limp hands and beamed at their daddy.

"These taxi drivers work so hard. Horan hasn't

seen his family for a month. You have given him this great opportunity to see them," Tau said.

Horan's wife brought a pile of cushions from a bedroom.

Leo and Allissa vacated the chair and slumped down on the piled-up cushions. Together they sat and listened to happy conversation they didn't understand. Tau sat on the opposite side of the room, shouting across some translations.

No one had slept enough in the last few days. They'd been constantly on edge, guessing and worrying about what was coming next. Right here, listening to the family whose brief unity they had caused, Leo felt the tight coils of pressure start to slowly unwind.

Through heavy eyes, Leo glanced from one person to the next. Some they'd just met, some they'd known for just a few days, but in the warmth of their company, he felt more comfortable than he had for a long time.

THE DAY of Mya's disappearance. Koh Tao, Thailand.

Five minutes must be up, Leo thought, turning his back on the water. The sea curled up behind him, and the stars led anywhere he could want to go. Tonight, however, he didn't want to be anywhere but here.

Koh Tao was beautiful, and to arrive with Mya was one of the most completing experiences of his life. The perfect place, he thought, remembering the warm shape of the ring in his palm.

The sound of the island intensified around him. Two animals yammered somewhere far off, sea and sand breathed together in harmony, and insects called to one another in the undergrowth.

Light from the windows of their cabin shimmered across the water. Somewhere up the road, a car started. Its engine whined for a moment before fading into the noises of the island.

Leo reached the cabin and looked back out across the water. He glanced above him and thought for a moment how strange it was that the same stars hung above his flat in Brighton each evening. Right now, that place and that life, seemed like a different planet entirely.

"I'm coming in," Leo said, reaching the door.

He braced himself, and pulled the door open. The room was how they'd left it. Their bags were dumped on the floor, with a few clothes piled on top. The bed was still made, just as it had been.

There was no sign of Mya.

Leo headed towards the bathroom. That was the only place she could possibly be.

"Hey, you're full of surprises tonight," he said, whispering into the door.

There was no reply.

"I'm coming in."

Leo turned the door handle. The door swung open slowly, showing Leo the bathroom inch by inch.

Leo held his breath. His chest tightened.

The bathroom was empty.

Mya had gone.

33

Dawn broke over the valley like it had every morning for fifty million years. Starting low, it lit a line between the uppermost mountain ridges and the sky. At first, a thin fracture in the darkness, which grew bigger with each moment until the tops of the mountains flared. The daylight then moved on to the lower slopes, lighting them each, one by one, the way an artist might paint a canvas.

Leo stood outside Horan's family home, looking across the tumbling landscape to the white peaks.

Sunrise is celebrated the world over for its beauty, its simplicity, and its inherent hope. This was the most hopeful sunrise Leo had seen in a long time.

Kathmandu and its slovenly passageways, hidden

restaurants, noise and dust, all seemed like a long way away.

"It's amazing what a bit of sleep can do," Allissa said, joining him and rubbing her eyes.

Her hair stood up on one side where she'd slept on his shoulder. He smiled as their elbows touched.

"This is not a bad place to wake up," Leo said.

"It's beautiful, isn't it?"

The morning had a cold, fresh bite.

"I think I could wake up here every morning and never get bored," Allissa said as a slither of sun appeared over the mountains.

Leo didn't reply. He was captivated by the scene.

A large bird pounded the still air.

The morning was fresh and innocent, but the day was coming. With each inch of the rising sun, the temperature would grow, people would wake, and traffic would rumble.

Voices came from the house. They spoke quickly, excitedly, until from outside they couldn't be distinguished from each other. The door opened, and Tau stepped out, he too rubbing sleep from his eyes.

"They're making us breakfast," he said. "Sleep alright?"

Leo and Allissa nodded and followed Tau inside.

Colorful plates and cups filled with a vegetable

soup, roti and milky sweet chai covered the table. It wasn't until Leo started to eat that he realized how hungry he was. The others felt the same and ate ravenously. Horan's mother refilled their bowls, and his wife brought more bread from the kitchen.

When they'd eaten all they could, Horan, Tau, Leo and Allissa made their way back to the vehicles. Horan went to get in the taxi.

"Let's take this one," Allissa said, pointing towards the Jeep. "Then when you've dropped us, it's yours."

Tau translated for Horan who beamed a smile. He didn't seem to care that the vehicle was stolen. Maybe that didn't matter so much this far from town, Leo thought, where was the nearest police station, anyway?

The friends received hugs and smiles from all members of Horan's family. Leo forced Horan's father to take some money for their hospitality and repairs for the taxi. Although he initially refused, Tau's encouragement eventually wore him down.

Leo slid into the Jeep. He longed for a shower. That was the first thing he'd do when they arrived in Pokhara. Horan started the engine, and they started down the track with Horan's family waving them goodbye.

The main road thronged with traffic. Cars, lorries and buses chugged past, bumper to bumper.

Leo glanced nervously at a river, hundreds of feet below the mountain road. If Horan was to slip, or one of the oncoming vehicles were to misjudge, the Jeep wouldn't stand a chance. Leo tried not to think of it and lay back, letting the wallowing vibrations of the journey relax him.

Six hours later, in the heat of the midday sun, they drove into Pokhara.

The Jeep crawled down a lakeside road surrounded by luscious, green, forest-covered hills. Pagodas stood out above the trees in glistening white and gold. Restaurants spilled onto wide pavements. Tourists sauntered beside the water.

"Right here," Tau said, directing them to a hotel.

They pulled up outside a white-painted building and got out of the car. Leo stretched his muscles back into use.

They'd offered Horan a night in the hotel, thinking he wouldn't want to make the return journey straight away, but he refused. Unloading their bags and pocketing the money and tip, Horan was back in the Jeep in less than three minutes.

Leo suspected he would use the extra money to

spend a few days with his family in their beautiful house. He deserved it.

Tau checked them into their rooms on the top floor overlooking the lake. Leo and Allissa were sharing a twin room, and Tau was next door. Leo and Allissa hadn't discussed sharing, but when the receptionist said that was all they had available, neither seemed to mind. Secretly, the thought of having company was welcomed by both.

Tau suggested they meet later for food. There were many good restaurants and bars in Pokhara, and they deserved a drink or three.

Leo and Allissa stumbled into the room and dropped their bags. Allissa lay on the bed nearest the door and Leo started the shower. Neither spoke.

While the shower ran hot, Leo charged his phone. It had died sometime in the last twenty-four hours without him even noticing.

As steam began to emanate from the bathroom door, Leo got up, undressed, and stepped beneath the jets, letting the water batter his skin. It enlivened and invigorated his senses. He washed quickly, then just stood there with the water running over him.

Leo's phone beeped several times from the bedroom. He ignored it.

Finally, he shut off the water, dried off, wrapped himself in a towel and padded back into the bedroom.

From the window, the blue surface of the lake skipped and shuddered in the early afternoon light. Beyond, the pine-covered hills sparkled in the haze.

Allissa had fallen asleep on one of the beds. Leo looked at her for a long moment. She had brought him here. Her tragedy, her grief, had now become twisted with his. Circumstances had muddled their lives without control.

Allissa turned in her sleep, her dark hair fanning across the pillow behind her.

Leo's phone beeped again. He picked it up from the pillow and collapsed backwards on to the bed. One text message was from his mum, one from his sister. Leo replied to them straight away, feeling guilty that he hadn't been in touch for a couple of days. The next message was from his Nepalese network provider. That was the sixth so far. Maybe these constant messages were how they justified their exorbitant charged.

The final message was from Stockwell. Leo opened the message. It was typically concise:

I know you have Allissa. I also have information you want. Let's arrange to meet when you're back.

Kathmandu Killers

It took Leo a few moments to see the attached picture.

His heart crawled up into his throat He jerked upright. His stomach made a fist. He had to see this.

He tapped on the icon and an image filled the screen. It was a face he hadn't seen for over two years. He instantly recognized the dark hair tied high, strong cheekbones, broad smile, big eyes. There was no doubt about it, it was a picture of Mya. And behind her, the unmistakable landscape of somewhere Leo knew she wanted to visit. Hong Kong.

34

Three days later. Brighton, England.

Leo crossed the apartment and gazed out of the large bay windows. Brighton was enjoying a momentary reprieve from the early winter weather. Although the sky was blue, it was cold outside. Leo pulled his hoodie tighter around him as a draft cut around the loose windows. A pair of seagulls leaped from the windowsill and wheeled, shrieking, into the air.

A sleek black car drew up outside. Leo couldn't recognize the brand from above, but the car gleamed. Ignoring all parking regulations, the car crossed a double-yellow line and bumped up the kerb.

The man-mountain, Giles, climbed out of the

passenger seat then opened the rear door. Stockwell clambered out, doing up his jacket.

Leo steadied his nerves. In the next few minutes, one way or another, this whole thing would be over.

Heavy footsteps thumped up the stairs, the sound carrying easily through the apartment's thin walls. Whoever converted the place from the grand Victorian house it once was, did so with the minimum of expense. Then, there it was. The heavy thumping at the door that had started this whole thing. This time Leo was prepared for the knock.

Leo sauntered to the front door. He wasn't going to rush. He wanted it to seem like he was in the middle of something important.

He opened the door the moment before Giles' giant fist was set to pound again. Without preamble Giles elbowed his way through.

Leo pointed out that all his electronics were on table in the front room, as they were last time. Giles again produced the hand-held bug detector and swept it across Leo's body. When he was clearly satisfied that Leo wasn't concealing any recording devices, he stepped into the kitchen.

Leo stood to the side as the giant man opened each cupboard, checked inside tins and ran the detector across the surfaces. As Leo had expected, this time

Stockwell was far more worried about things being overheard.

"All clear," Giles said into the hidden comms device.

Leo stepped into the kitchen and busied himself making coffee. He didn't really want the drink, but just wanted something to keep his hands still. By the time Lord Stockwell arrived, hissing and wheezing from the climb up the stairs, Leo had almost finished preparing the coffee.

"Where is she?" Stockwell said, beady eyes moving from one side of the room to the next. Now that Leo had what he wanted, The Lord was clearly dispensing with all niceties.

"Want coffee?" Leo pointed at the two cups he'd lined up on the counter.

"I want you to tell me where my daughter is."

Leo swallowed the tiny flicker of anxiety which threatened to rise within him. He had been over this conversation several times and knew exactly how it was going to go.

"I've got a few questions for you first," Leo said, pouring milk and hot water into both cups anyway. "I expect you're surprised to see me back here again?"

"No, not at all. Why would I be?" Stockwell spat in reply.

"You see Lord Stockwell, I've done a fair bit of research about you since we last met. There certainly is more to you than meets the eye, isn't there?"

"I have no idea. I sent you to go and find my daughter. She was missing, and I was worried about her, like any father would be."

"Yes of course, you were worried about her. You were particularly worried about her, though, because of what she knew. Isn't that so?"

"Young man, I have no idea what you're talking about, but you're this close to me walking out of here with everything I know about your friend Mya." Stockwell held his finger and thumb together in a visual demonstration of how close Leo was.

Leo worked hard to keep his face emotionless at the mention of Mya's name. He wasn't certain he'd got away with it, until he saw the slight narrowing of the other man's eyes.

"I don't think that would be wise," Leo said, opening a drawer and removing a yellow folder. "You see, when I met Allissa, she told me the real reason she didn't want anything to do with you. It seems she overheard a conversation you had with your wife some years ago. She's written all about it in this statement." Leo read a section of the statement, detailing the admissions contained within the conversation.

Stockwell paled. He moved his lips like he had a really bad taste in his mouth. Leo could almost see the cogs of his mind whirring, searching for a solution.

"With my encouragement Allissa has passed this statement to the police. She's also indicated that when this goes to court, she'll be willing testify."

Stockwell snatched the statement from Leo's grasp. His piggy eyes moved across the page.

"This means nothing."

Although Stockwell sounded confident, Leo detected the slightest hint of doubt.

"The lunatic ravings of a troubled young woman," Stockwell said.

"I'm not sure the judge will see it that way," Leo said.

Stockwell grinned, then slammed the statement down on the counter top. "Mr Keane, you'll have to do better than that. You've got nothing. Plus, I know half the judges in this country. This would be thrown out of court in moments. No judge or jury will believe that."

"I'll testify too, and say that you set us up to be killed in Kathmandu. I bet there is some kind of phone record."

"Of course there's not. Do you really think..." Stockwell mocked, stopping himself mid sentence.

"You knew the operation that those men were running in that restaurant, you set us up to go there." Leo's voice increased in pitch. He felt his temperature rise and his face flush.

Stockwell tilted his head to the side. "Mr Keane, I have no idea what you're talking about. It was good working with you, but we're done here." Stockwell turned towards the door.

"One more thing," Leo said, trying to ignore the sensation that it was all slipping away from him. "How did you know that I would end up finding Allissa?"

Stockwell swung back around and pointed a finger at Leo. "You see Mr Keane, there are two types of people in a society like ours. There are those that succeed." Stockwell pointed the finger at himself. "And there are those that fail. These people who fail can't help themselves. They fail, and they fail, and they fail, and there's nothing to be done about it. Unfortunately for you, Mr Keane, you are one of those failures. And, unfortunately for me, my daughter likes to associate with people like that. She's what I think you call a "fixer". She wants to do good all the time." Now warm to his theme, Stockwell rambled on. "It's such a frustrating habit. I don't know where she gets it from. Anyway, I knew you'd go out there, I knew you'd stumble your way into each other somehow, and I knew, when suggested, you'd wander along to that damn restaurant. You're just too predictable. Then, of course, my problems would be solved." Stockwell brushed his hands together. "On that, I'm afraid I must go." Stockwell looked around the kitchen as though it was museum reconstruction entitled 'the lives of common people.'

"It didn't work, though, did it?" Leo said, a sharp edge to his voice. "Allissa and I are here, we made it out alive, and we will tear down everything that you've done, piece by piece."

Fury burned in Stockwell's eyes. Leo was clearly getting to him, which was exactly what he intended to do. "Don't think, for a moment, that because you got lucky once, that changes anything. If I were you, I would run, run as fast and as far as you can. I wish I could deal with you right now, but that would raise far too many questions." Spittle flew from Stockwell's lips. "But I'll find you, I'll track you down. Running will only buy you time. I'll come for you, and I'll find you. At least if you run now, you'll enjoy the last few weeks of your pathetic little life."

Leo stepped across to the kitchen wall and banged three times. "Is that enough?" he said out loud. Feet shuffled on the floor above.

Stockwell glanced at the ceiling, confused.

"That's the thing with these converted properties, there really was no expense spent," Leo said. "I often joke that I can hear my neighbors upstairs changing their minds."

Footsteps thudded down the staircase now.

Stockwell looked as though he was trying to swallow a dozen wasps.

"They'll have heard everything you said, recorded it too," Leo concluded, folding his arms. "I guess that's what you call, game over."

35

"I guess that's what you call game over?" Allissa said. "I can't believe you actually said that. Do you think you're the Terminator or something?"

They were walking down Brighton Seafront wrapped up against the cold wind which hurled itself in from the sea.

"Yeah. I sort of hope they don't play that bit in court. I couldn't think of anything else to say, you know, to sort of sum it up."

Allissa stopped at the railing and turned out to face the water. Joined by a pair of police officers, Allissa had heard the whole conversation from Leo's neighbor's kitchen. When the officers had charged down to make the arrest, Allissa had stayed upstairs.

She didn't want to see Stockwell a moment before it was absolutely necessary.

"What're you going to do now?" Leo said, standing beside Allissa at the railing. Traffic rumbled along the promenade behind them.

"Probably go and find somewhere for lunch. Maybe have a beer too. I'll buy you one, I suppose it's the least I can do." Allissa pointed towards the city center further down the seafront.

"That's not really what I meant," Leo said, pulling a lungful of the salty air. He felt out of shape. Now he was back in Brighton, he was looking forward to running again. "I mean after that, where are you going to go now?"

"Oh, right," Allissa said. "I'm not sure. Hadn't thought about it. Go back to Kathmandu, I suppose." Her hands gripped the railing more firmly at the thought.

A wave, larger than most, crashed against the stones.

Leo frowned. *I could just ask her, couldn't I?*

His mouth formed the shape of the words, but no sound came out.

"You could..." he started, stopping again as he heard the words stumble out.

"What?"

"You could stay here for a bit if you like. I have a spare room."

Allissa thought for a moment and then turned to face Leo. "You know what, that doesn't sound like a totally terrible idea."

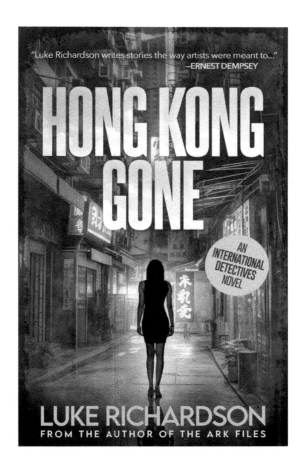

Dream job to living nightmare...

Isobel's move to Hong Kong is supposed to be a dream come true. When she witnesses a murder and becomes entangled in a deadly plot, she realizes she's isolated, vulnerable and a long way from home.

Detectives Leo and Allissa, fresh from solving a case in Kathmandu, are immediately put to the test.

Their mission: find Isobel, who has vanished without a trace in a city where danger lurks around every corner.

The minutes tick by and Isobel's window for escape narrows. As Leo and Allissa try to navigate a maze of lies and corruption, Leo faces a shocking personal revelation, and the line between the hunters and the hunted blurs.

HONG KONG GONE is the second electrifying instalment in Luke Richardson's International Detectives Thriller Series. For fans of relentless suspense and heart-stopping twists, this is a sequel that promises to be as compelling as it is unpredictable.

Search your local Amazon store, your favourite bookseller, or ask in your library for **Hong Kong Gone by Luke Richardson.**

www.lukerichardsonauthor.com/hongkong

Hong Kong

A dream proposal turns into a heart-stopping nightmare when Leo's fiancée vanishes without a trace in the tropical paradise of Koh Tao.

Travelling the world with the love of his life, Leo's looking for the perfect place to propose. Reaching the Thai tropical paradise of Koh Tao, he thinks he's found it.

But before he gets an answer, she's nowhere to be seen.

On searching the resort, his tranquillity turns to turmoil. What began as a dream escape swiftly spirals into a harrowing quest as he must to work out whether this is a practical joke gone wrong, or something much more sinister.

Discover where it all began in KOH TAO BETRAYAL, the compelling introduction to Luke Richardson's Bestselling International Detective Series.

Grab your FREE copy now!
www.lukerichardsonauthor.com/kohtao

AUTHOR'S NOTE

This book is dedicated to all those I've traveled beside.

First, foremost and always, Mark and Valerie, Mum and Dad. Your sense of courage and adventure is my inspiration.

Thank you for reading my first novel. The completion of this book is the dream of many years.

The story of the lamb and the restaurant has been going around in my mind for a long time. So long, in fact, that I can't remember how I first came across it. But it wasn't until I visited Kathmandu that I put the two together, along with our nervous investigator, Leo.

As may come across in my writing, traveling,

exploring and seeing the world is so important to me, as is coming home to my family and friends.

I visited Kathmandu in 2016 and found it such an interesting place that it inspired this book.

During the Hippy Trail of the 60s and 70s, Kathmandu was a popular destination for young travelers seeking spiritual enlightenment and an escape from the conventional life. The overland route from Europe to India and Nepal saw thousands of adventurous souls making their way through countries like Turkey, Iran, Afghanistan, Pakistan, and India before finally reaching Kathmandu.

The city's laid-back atmosphere, coupled with the availability of cheap accommodation and relaxed drug laws, made it an attractive place for these "hippies" to gather. Many were drawn to the exotic culture, the stunning natural beauty of the Himalayas, and the promise of spiritual awakening.

Freak Street, once the heart of the hippie community in Kathmandu, was lined with guesthouses, cafes, and shops catering to the needs of free-spirited travelers. It was a place where East met West—the scent of incense mingling with the sound of rock music.

The influx of hippies had a significant impact on the local culture and economy, with many Nepalese

Author's Note

adapting to cater to the tastes and needs of these visitors. However, the Hippy Trail came to an end in the late 1970s due to political instability in the region and the increasing availability of cheap air travel.

Today, Kathmandu continues to be a popular destination for travelers, although the nature of tourism has changed since the days of the Hippy Trail. While some visitors still come seeking spiritual experiences, many are drawn to the city's rich cultural heritage, vibrant festivals, and opportunities for adventure sports like trekking, mountain biking, and white-water rafting in the nearby mountains.

I also touch upon the struggles of the some of the local people in this book. Whilst visiting, I learned of the shockingly common practice of women and girls being taken to city with the promise of jobs and opportunities which end up in domestic slavery or prostitution. There are now several charities dedicated to this cause, should you want to learn more.

Strangely enough, the idea of the backstreet restaurant came to me during a previous trip to Bangkok, Thailand. One evening a friend and I visited a nightclub on the recommendation of a pair of fellow travelers. We had a great evening, dancing the night away, drinking Chang Beer and meeting people from all around the world. In the morning, discussing the night before, we both remembered the name of the nightclub, but not its location. Ultimately, we turned to our guidebook for the answer. The guidebook said something like:

The nightclub seems to only exist during the hours of darkness. The only people who know exactly where it is are the taxi and tuktuk drivers. A Bangkok must do, if you can find it.

As such, the idea of the backstreet restaurant—although mine was a lot more sinister—was born.

As the first that I wrote and published, this book was far from perfect in its initial incarnation. I have re-edited it and re-published it since then, tightening up the story to make it closer to the "thriller" style books I now love to read and write. I think this is quite common with new writers—we set out with the aim of "writing something" without really knowing what we want that thing to be.

My re-edit of the book in 2023, four years after its publication, was generally met with kind comments from readers. Some, however, were so keen on the original version that they didn't want it to change. Should you be interested in the original version, I have made it available here: www.lukerichardsonauthor.com/kathmanduoriginal

Author's Note

Of course, I am still immensely proud of this book and hope you enjoy it too. Although the words here are my own, the characters, experiences and some of the events described are wholly inspired by the people I've traveled beside.

If we ever shared noodles from a street-food vendor, visited a temple together, played cards on a creaking overnight train, or had a beer in a back-street restaurant, you are forever in this book, and for that, I thank you!

It is the intention of my writing to show that although the world is big and the unknown can be unsettling, there is so much good in it. Although the men in the restaurant and people traffickers are bad, evil people, I think they are vastly outnumbered by the honesty, purity and kindness of the other characters. You don't have to look far to see this in the real world. I know that whenever I'm on the road, it's the kindness of the people that I remember, almost more than the place itself.

Whether you're an experienced traveler, or you prefer your home turf, I hope this story has taken you somewhere new and exciting—even if you've been to Kathmandu and found the backstreet restaurant.

Again, thank you for coming on the adventure with me. I hope to see you again.

Luke

(March 2019 and rewritten in April 2023)

PS. A little warning, next time someone talks to you on the road, be careful what you say, as you may end up in their book.

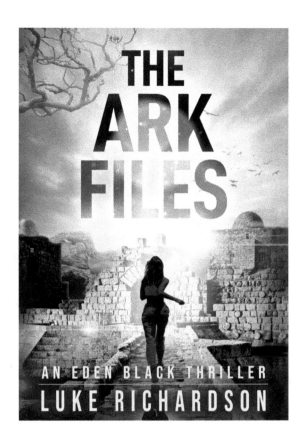

A secret society...
An ancient manuscript...
One woman to save the world...

Professional treasure hunter EDEN BLACK is no stranger to action. After all, the artifacts she spends her life returning to their rightful owners aren't always easy to access.

When Eden's father dies in a plane crash, her life's turned upside down. Grief turns to fear when she learns that it wasn't an accident. Everyone involved in an archaeological dig twenty years ago has met with a similar untimely end. Everyone that is, but Eden who was ten at the time.

When her father's house is raided and burned to the ground, Eden's forced into action. To learn the truth about her father's death and save herself from sharing his fate, Eden must uncover the manuscript and expose its secrets once and for all.

But this time the world is watching, and not everyone is on her side.

THE ARK FILES is the first in a brand-new pulse-pounding archaeological thriller series by Luke Richardson. Fans of Dan Brown, Clive Cussler, and Ernest Dempsey will devour this in hours!

Have you met Eden Black?

www.lukerichardsonauthor.com/arkfiles

Or search your local Amazon store, your favourite bookseller, or ask in your local library for **The Ark Files by Luke Richardson.**

www.ingramcontent.com/pod-product-compliance
Ingram Content Group UK Ltd.
Pitfield, Milton Keynes, MK11 3LW, UK
UKHW021422070725
6762UKWH00033B/1109